"I'm not goi ⬛⬛⬛ **"
Jared said. "** ⬛⬛⬛
just want to k ⬛⬛⬛
you."

It wasn't the ⬛⬛⬛⬛⬛ ⬛⬛⬛, for she bristled immediately. "I don't need taking care of."

Her reaction surprised him. All he wanted was to help . . . and maybe enjoy the pleasure of holding her for a while. It had been so long since he'd held a woman in his arms. "Maybe you're fine, but I'm not. I'm wet and cold, and I'm going over there." He pointed to the back of the cave. "If you want to join me, fine. If not, fine. It's your decision."

He found a comfortable spot and settled down, his back against the wall. He was soaked and freezing and knew she must be too. Laurie remained standing, staring out at the rain. Finally she walked over to him.

"I decided you're right. We can keep each other warm," she said, and sat. Having her next to him instantly increased his body temperature. Her shoulder touched his arm, and he breathed in deeply, enjoying her sweet, feminine scent. A shiver shook his body, and she looked at him.

"You are cold, aren't you?"

"I'll live."

She snuggled closer and slipped an arm around his waist. "How's that?"

He groaned softly. "Much warmer." He felt her touching him everywhere.

Her voice was shaky as he snuggled her closer. "Maybe we could talk."

"I don't want to talk," Jared said softly. "I want to kiss you." He didn't know if it was the cave or the cold, but he felt a primitive desire to protect, to possess this woman, to make her his. . . .

WHAT ARE *LOVESWEPT* ROMANCES?

They are stories of true romance and touching emotion. We believe those two very important ingredients are constants in our highly sensual and very believable stories in the *LOVESWEPT* line. Our goal is to give you, the reader, stories of consistently high quality that may sometimes make you laugh, sometimes make you cry, but are always fresh and creative and contain many delightful surprises within their pages.

Most romance fans read an enormous number of books. Those they truly love, they keep. Others may be traded with friends and soon forgotten. We hope that each *LOVESWEPT* romance will be a treasure—a "keeper." We will always try to publish

LOVE STORIES YOU'LL NEVER FORGET
BY AUTHORS YOU'LL ALWAYS REMEMBER

The Editors

Maris Soule
Jared's Lady

BANTAM BOOKS
NEW YORK · TORONTO · LONDON · SYDNEY · AUCKLAND

JARED'S LADY

A Bantam Book / January 1992

*If you would be interested in receiving protective vinyl
covers for your Loveswept books, please write to this address
for information:*

> *Loveswept*
> *Bantam Books*
> *P.O. Box 985*
> *Hicksville, NY 11802*

ISBN 0-553-44179-5

Published simultaneously in the United States and Canada

*Bantam Books are published by Bantam Books, a division
of Bantam Doubleday Dell Publishing Group, Inc. Its trademark, consisting of the words "Bantam Books" and the
portrayal of a rooster, is Registered in U.S. Patent and
Trademark Office and in other countries. Marca Registrada.
Bantam Books, 666 Fifth Avenue, New York, New York 10103.*

PRINTED IN THE UNITED STATES OF AMERICA

OPM   0 9 8 7 6 5 4 3 2 1

Dedicated to my folks.

One

Ominous, dark clouds hung low over the hills of southern Illinois. The humidity was high, the air dead still, and the black-and-white cattle grazing by an old, weather-beaten barn watched a dozen men and women walk through a field of chest-high corn. Frantically each called out the same name.

"Susie!"

From inside the barn and the sheds around the white two-story farmhouse others echoed the name, while in the yard two men hunched over a map spread across the hood of a sheriff's patrol car.

Sheriff Roger Olsen wore the regulation brown uniform of the Norton Sheriff's Department. The shirt stuck to his sweat-dampened back, while the trousers clung to his long, thin legs. Jared North was shorter and broader built than the sheriff, and his dark gray suit jacket and red-and-black-striped tie lay on the roof of the patrol car. The sleeves of his white shirt were rolled to his elbows. He nervously ran his fingers through his thick blond hair, then began chewing on the end of his pen.

Neither man noticed when one more car pulled into the yard and a woman and her dog got out.

"I don't think Susie could get to that pond in the pasture," Jared was saying, "and I looked all around it for her shoe prints, but I don't know, Roger." The idea of his niece being at the bottom of the murky gray-green pool of water tightened the knot in Jared's gut. "Do you think we should dredge it?"

"Don't go lookin' for the worst, Jer," the sheriff said. "Let's just wait and see what that tracking dog finds. Laurie should be here soon."

"I'm here and ready to go to work."

At the sound of a soft, feminine voice, Jared turned from the car and map. Before him stood a miniature-sized woman, the top of her head barely reaching his shoulders. She carried an orange, coated-cloth gear bag on her back, and a bright-orange vest covered her chest. The rest of her uniform was comprised of a khaki blouse and slacks and tiny, almost doll-like, scuffed brown hiking boots.

The moment he spun around, she gasped and brought her hand to her mouth. Her gaze leaped from his eyes to his hair, then down to his shoulders.

If there was something about blue eyes, blond hair, and broad shoulders that surprised her, Jared wasn't sure what. He knew he'd never met her before, and if either of them should be shocked, it should be he.

When Roger had said there was a local woman who had a tracking dog and suggested calling her, Jared had expected a woman of some stature, a woman who could handle a dog, hike up and down the steep hills of the rugged countryside, and be a help in this search.

Instead he was looking at a woman who wasn't much bigger than his missing niece. She might be in her twenties, but she looked like a kid, especially with her damp brown hair pulled back in a ponytail and wearing no makeup. Even her voice had sounded like a child's—sweet and small. And he was sure she couldn't weight more than the huge black German shepherd sitting by her side. Panting, its long tongue hanging out and its bright white teeth showing, the animal looked formidable and, without the orange harness and leash, could have been mistaken for a small black bear.

"Thanks for coming so quickly, Laurie," Roger said. After another puzzled glance at Jared the woman turned to the sheriff. "Jared says you've never met. So, Jared North meet Laurie Crawford. And vice versa."

She extended her hand. "You're the missing girl's father?"

"No, Susie's uncle." He took her hand, and her slender fingers almost disappeared in his grasp. Her shake, however, was quite firm. He liked that.

"Tom Meinstra's out of town attending a growers' seminar," the sheriff explained. "So far we haven't been able to get hold of him. The mother, Jared's sister, is in the house. She had a baby just a little over a week ago. She's taking this as well as can be expected."

He bent over to pat the head of the German shepherd. "And this is the Captain, Jared. Otherwise known as Cappie. You're a good dog, aren't you, boy."

The black dog wagged his tail and cocked his head to the side so Roger could scratch the thick ruff of double-layered hair around his neck. Jared watched for a moment, then his gaze returned to the woman.

Even though she had brown hair and brown eyes—not blond and blue—she continued to remind him of his niece. He'd call Laurie Crawford cute. Maybe even sexy. The words that didn't come to mind were strong, capable, or self-sufficient. Abruptly he turned to the sheriff. "Rog, we need to talk. Privately."

Before the man had a chance to say anything, Jared steered him away from the car and Laurie and over toward the house. "It won't work," he said flatly.

"What won't work?"

"We can't send that woman out." He nodded in Laurie's direction. "Look at her. She's no bigger than a child."

The sheriff looked, and so did Jared. Laurie was standing where they'd left her, the black dog still sitting by her side. She gave them a quick, acknowledging smile. The sheriff returned it; Jared didn't. He had to make Roger understand his concern. "She can't—"

He was interrupted by the screen door to the house opening. A middle-age woman stuck her head out and yelled, "Sheriff, telephone call."

Roger grimaced, his glance swinging indecisively from Laurie to the woman, then back to Laurie. Finally he made up his mind. "Let me get this call, Jer, then we'll talk about her."

Jared didn't want to wait for a telephone conversation. Time was too precious. But Roger walked away, leaping up the porch steps and disappearing into the house.

"What seems to be the problem, Mr. North?"

Jared jerked his gaze downward and to the side. How quickly he'd come to recognize Laurie's soft voice, he mused. And how quietly she and her dog had walked up beside him.

Perhaps it was better to speak to her, explain his concerns. "There's a thunderstorm headed this way."

She nodded, glancing at the fast-moving, dark clouds above them. "A bad one from what I've heard."

She didn't understand.

He didn't understand himself why he was so worried about a complete stranger, but he was. "I don't think it would be safe for you to go looking for my niece. What if the storm hits while you're out? Besides the lightning, I've heard it has winds over forty miles an hour."

He couldn't stop himself from once again scanning her figure. Quickly, but she noticed none the less, and when he looked at her face, she was grinning. "Believe it or not," she said, "I've never been blown away by a strong wind."

He obviously wasn't getting his point across. "There are also reports of hail as big as golf balls. This search could very quickly turn dangerous."

"I've been trained to deal with all types of situations, including bad weather. To be certified, both my dog and I have had to go through a rigorous training process and pass procedural tests." She patted her dog's head. "We'll know what to do if the storm hits."

Even if she and her dog knew what to do, Jared thought, on a night like this the Shawnee Hills were no place for a woman who couldn't possibly top five feet or one hundred pounds. He touched her arm. He wasn't sure why. Perhaps to see just how tiny she felt. Perhaps because ever since she'd shaken his hand, he'd wanted to touch her again, feel her warmth, her vitality.

That he found her attractive bothered him. Susie was missing. That was the only thing he should be thinking about. Not how Laurie Crawford's eyes were as dark as pure cocoa, her lashes long and lush, her lips perfectly shaped.

The first rumble of thunder sounded in the distance. Jared jerked his hand back, stunned that he had let his thoughts stray—even for a moment—from finding Susie. "We need to get started."

"I agree." Laurie looked toward the house. "I hope the sheriff doesn't take much longer."

"Listen, why don't you stay here . . . with my sister. Let Roger and me take your dog out."

"You'll take the Captain?" She laughed. "And what do you know about search-and-rescue procedures, Mr. North? What do you know about tracking dogs?"

She had him there. He knew absolutely nothing about dogs in general, let alone tracking dogs. "Well . . ."

"Well, nothing." She placed a hand on his arm, just above his wrist, her touch light yet caressing. "I appreciate your concern for my safety, but don't worry. I'll be fine."

"How do you keep up with your dog?"

"I don't have to. Cappie works off lead. When he makes a find, he comes back and takes me to it. I can get where I need to go fast enough."

He hoped so.

She dropped her hand, and he instantly missed the physical contact. She kept looking at him, though, deep into his eyes, and he'd describe her expression as questioning. Maybe even interested.

Another time, another place, and he'd be interested himself, but right now, finding Susie was more important. He glanced toward the field behind the house, and Laurie's gaze followed his.

"Do you have any idea where your niece went?" she asked.

"No."

"Have you searched the woods?"

Roger Olsen had asked the same question earlier. Jared gave the same answer. "No. I'm sure Susie wouldn't go there."

"Why not?"

"Because she was told not to."

Once again Laurie laughed.

He didn't know why she laughed. His sister and

brother-in-law's farm was right in the midst of the Shawnee National Forest. The woods on the other side of the hay field were part of a section two miles square, and no place for a child to play. They'd repeatedly told Susie that.

It was the pond that worried him. Susie loved to swim.

And it was hot.

The screen door opened, and the sheriff came back out. "Sorry for the delay," he said, his long legs quickly carrying him across the porch and down the steps. "Accident north of town. Nothing too serious from the sound of it, but I had to make sure everything was under control. Isn't this typical? I can go all week without a call, then when it rains, it pours."

Another distant rumble of thunder made the cliché ominous.

Roger stopped beside Laurie, but looked at Jared. "Now, what was the problem you wanted to discuss?"

"I don't think she should go," Jared said. It was as simple as that. "She's too—"

There were a lot of words he could use to describe Laurie and explain his concern. She was too small. Too defenseless. Too young. Too vulnerable. Too pretty. She could turn into a liability, not an asset. Maybe, if sheer grit were enough, she wouldn't have any problems; but he'd learned from Joann, his late wife, that grit and determination didn't always make a difference when it came to life-and-death situations.

"Too small," he finally finished.

"My size shouldn't have anything to do with this." Laurie glared at him, her cocoa eyes turning stormy, those tempting lips thinning to a firm, unyielding line. Then, with a flip of her ponytail, she faced the sheriff. "Do you want my dog's help or not?"

"Jer, what's wrong with you?" Roger asked. "You want to find your niece, don't you?"

"Of course I do."

"Then I agree with her. Her size isn't important." He looked back at Laurie. "I'll give you a quick rundown of what's happened."

Jared didn't know what else to say. The decision had been made, and from the look of disdain Laurie shot him, his effort to protect her had put him at the top of her most unwanted list. Any thoughts, no matter how fleeting, he'd had about asking her out seemed irrelevant.

He only half-listened to what Roger was telling her. He already knew the story. His sister had been outside playing with Susie when the baby woke and started crying. Becky went in to change him, and when she came back out, Susie was gone. Becky called around the house, checked every place she could imagine a five-year-old might hide, then phoned him—half hysterical. He came out as quickly as he could.

During the drive from Norton to the farm, he had been sure Susie was simply hiding. Becky had said the girl had been jealous over all the attention the baby was getting. What better way to be noticed than to make your mother think you were lost? He was certain once Susie heard his voice, she'd come out. The child adored him. She always came running when she saw him.

But not today.

He searched for over an hour before giving up and calling for help. Roger Olsen had arrived almost immediately, organizing Becky's friends and neighbors to help. So far, though, no one had found any sign of the child, and Jared didn't know what else to do or where else to look. If this didn't start him smoking again, nothing would.

"The child's now been missing nearly three

hours," the sheriff said, bringing Laurie up-to-date.

"Have you ruled out the possibility of a kidnapping?" she asked.

Jared answered the question. "I didn't even consider it at first, and the neighbors I talked to said they didn't see any unfamiliar people or cars on the road this afternoon, but now I'm beginning to think it's a possibility."

He was sure no one would kidnap Susie to get money from Tom and Becky. Although the farm was doing well, his sister and brother-in-law weren't rich. No, if anyone had taken Susie, it would be to get to him. Maybe Norton was a small town, but his company, North Machinery, was known nationwide for its innovative machinery designs and excellence in manufacturing. Not long ago, the Harrisburg *Daily Register* had run an article about how the company had grown since George North retired and his son Jared took control. The article had mentioned Becky and Tom and their daughter, Susie. Some nut could have read it and decided kidnapping Jared North's niece would be an easy way to make money.

He prayed that wasn't the case.

"The child is five?" Laurie asked.

"Just." Jared remembered Susie's party. "Her birthday was June sixth." The day he'd stopped smoking.

"What was she wearing the last time she was seen?"

"Her mother described her clothing," Roger said, and relayed the information.

Anxious and restless, Jared glanced around. People were everywhere, in the fields, searching through the barn and outbuildings, around the tractors and harvest machinery. They were at least doing something. He hadn't felt this helpless since his wife had died.

Laurie continued asking questions about Susie, and Roger gave her answers from the notes he'd taken earlier. To Jared it all seemed a waste of time. "Look," he interrupted finally, "you already know I don't think you should leave this yard, Miss Crawford, but if we're going to use your dog, shouldn't we get started?"

She faced him, her expression stony. "Mr. North, the time I take now, asking these questions, may very well save your niece's life later."

"Or," he countered, his temper rising with his anxiety, "we may end up abandoning the whole damn search because it's so dark we can't see two feet in front of us."

She glanced at the sky, checked her watch, then turned her back on him and spoke to the sheriff. "Do you have something of the child's that Cappie can get a scent from?"

"Her mother gave me a sweater the girl had on early this morning, before it got so danged hot and humid." Roger wiped his sweat-dampened forehead with his arm, then started for the porch railing, where a child's sweater hung.

"Wait! Don't touch it," Laurie ordered.

Roger stopped. She slipped the orange gear bag from her shoulders, zipped it open, and removed a plastic bag. "Put the sweater in this. We don't want to touch it any more than necessary."

"You're too late," Jared said. "My sister and I already handled that sweater." Preserving a fresh scent hadn't crossed his mind when he'd picked the sweater up from the ground and handed it to his sister.

He watched the sheriff carefully place the sweater into the plastic bag. Laurie took the bag and held it open in front of her dog.

The Captain sniffed.

It was then that Becky Meinstra stepped out from the house onto the porch, the screen door banging shut behind her. "Jared, what's going on?"

His sister's figure still showed the signs of her recent pregnancy, and she carried her newborn son in her arms. She looked tired and strung out, and her eyes were red-rimmed from crying. Sometimes Jared envied a woman's freedom to cry. Not that he'd never cried. His had just been done in private.

"We're letting the dog smell Susie's sweater," he said, and walked up onto the porch. "How are you doing?"

"Okay. . . . Mildred Weisop helped me change Todd, and Irene's fixing some soup. Any sign of Susie?"

"None yet, but we'll find her soon."

He put an arm around her shoulders and hugged her. People said there was no doubting Becky and he were related. He didn't see it. Becky was pretty; at best he'd call his looks striking. Before the baby she'd had a nice figure. He looked like a triangle on its apex. They did both have blue eyes and blond hair, although he kept finding white hairs in his. If he had to go through many more days like this one, he wouldn't be surprised if his turned completely white.

"We'll find her," he repeated, and gave Becky's shoulders another gentle squeeze. She wasn't the only one he was trying to convince. He couldn't imagine what he'd do if anything happened to his niece. Susie had become the little girl he'd always wished Joann and he could have had.

His sister looked at the German shepherd, then at Laurie. "She's so small," she whispered.

"I know," he grumbled.

"Miss," Becky called, "do you really think you and your dog can find my little girl?"

"We've found missing children before." Laurie closed the plastic bag, told her dog to stay, then walked over and introduced herself. "Laurie Craw-ford. Co-owner of LaRu's Pet Shop. Where exactly did you last see your daughter?"

"Over there, by the swings." Becky pointed to the swing set by the side of the house. "It was some-time between four-thirty and five. After I changed Todd, I was going to fix dinner, and Susie was going to help me. I just thought she'd stay there, on the swing. I never thought she'd . . ."

Tears filled her eyes again, and Jared hugged her close. He'd never handled a woman's crying well. Not his mother's. Not Becky's. Not Joann's. It tore at his insides, made him feel helpless.

Only, right now he had to be strong. Becky—and Susie—were depending on him. He knew what to do for Becky. His sister needed rest. "Go back inside, Beck. Lie down. We're going to get the dog started. I'll let you know when we find her."

"You ready?" the sheriff asked Laurie.

"Ready as I'll ever be, I suppose." Laurie picked up her gear bag and slipped it on her back. "Will you be going with me?"

Roger shook his head. "I've got to wait for the park rangers to show up. I'll pull a deputy and send him with you."

The sheriff had only two deputies. One was with the search party in the cornfield and the other was leading the search through the barn and sheds. Although Jared didn't think either would find his niece in those areas, he also couldn't see any sense in taking them away from their jobs. Dropping his arm from his sister's shoulders, he straightened. "You don't need to pull anyone, Roger. I'm going with her."

"Good," Becky said with a sigh.

Laurie's expression stated otherwise. "We don't take family members with us when we go out. Your scent might confuse my dog."

"Why my scent? It's not like I'm around Susie all

the time." In fact he hadn't spent much time with her lately. Now he wished he had.

"All right," Laurie said, "maybe in your case your scent wouldn't confuse Cappie, but I can't have someone with me who's going to get emotional and fall apart."

"Do I look the type who gets emotional and falls apart?"

She stared at him for a moment, then tried again. "What I need is a partner who's had some training in rescue procedures."

"I've taken CPR and the Red Cross first-aid classes."

If that impressed her, she didn't show it. "More specifically I need someone who can follow orders. Someone who can handle a radio if necessary, read a map. Someone who'll help me look for signs of your niece."

"I can do all that."

Her gaze darted down, over his white shirt and suit pants to his black leather shoes. "You're not dressed appropriately."

What he was wearing had been right for his office, and when Becky called, he hadn't thought to swing by his house to change. Since nothing of Tom's would fit him, he wasn't going to worry about his shoes and clothes. Finding Susie was more important than his wardrobe. "I'll manage."

Once again her eyes locked with his. He knew she didn't want him with her. Her answer confirmed it. "No. I'd be better off on my own."

This time he wasn't giving in. He stepped down off the porch and strode toward her. "Look, we're wasting time again. I'm going with you, and that's it. So let's get going."

"I'm not going to argue with you," she said, standing firm. "You're not going."

"Arguing is exactly what you're doing," Jared pointed out. "And it's going to be dark soon."

"Take him, Laurie," Roger said, ending the debate. "I know this guy pretty well. He might be a little bullheaded at times, but he won't hinder you. Plus, I think you'll end up in one of the areas we're already checking."

She obviously wasn't happy about it, but she gave in. "Then you do exactly as I say," she said to Jared. "Do you understand? No interfering with my dog. No getting in my way."

"I wouldn't think of interfering." He ran a large, successful company; he knew how to supervise without interfering.

"Okay, let me give my dog one more sniff of that sweater, then I'll give him the command to track."

She headed for the swing set, her dog by her side. Knowing he was about to start, the shepherd was no longer quiet. Prancing and wagging his tail, he watched every move Laurie made.

Roger patted the two-way radio hanging from his belt. "I'll let you know when the rangers arrive, Jared."

"And we'll keep in touch," Jared said, as much for his sister's peace of mind as for Roger's information.

The sheriff nodded, but Laurie looked back, and Jared caught the full force of her glare. Apparently, he realized, she considered his answering for her as interfering. As prickly and defensive as she was, he wondered why he'd thought her attractive.

Two

Stopping at the swing set, Laurie let the German shepherd smell Susie's sweater one more time, then she released his leash. "Track 'em!" she ordered.

The dog barked excitedly, spun around, and trotted away from the swing. As the Captain ranged out in a large circle, sniffing the air and checking the yard, Laurie gave no commands, no directions. After making several wide circles, the dog padded into the hay field.

That surprised Jared; he'd looked there earlier. Not thoroughly, certainly, but he had walked up the hill some, and so had others. None of them had found any signs of Susie, and it didn't seem reasonable that a five-year-old would climb the hill. All that was on the other side was the forbidden woods . . . and rocks.

But the dog continued in that direction.

Laurie sent a mock salute to the sheriff, then looked at Jared. She didn't say a word, but when she turned and started after her dog, he was certain she hoped he'd stay where he was.

He did for a couple of minutes, seeing no need to move if the dog was simply going to go up, then head back down. Laurie had hiked a good quarter of the way up the hill before he realized the Captain wasn't coming back. The pair were headed for the trees.

_"Damn!" Jared muttered, and glanced back at his sister. She was staring after the dog, crying softly as she rocked the baby in her arms.

"Looks like Susie went into the forest after all," Roger Olsen said, coming up next to Jared. "Hope those rangers get here soon."

"I can't believe she'd do that, not after all the lectures her father and I gave her."

"Kids do strange things."

Laurie was near the top of the hill now. She paused and looked back at the house, then continued following her dog.

"She's not going to wait for you," Roger said. "If you're going, Jer, you'd better get."

"I still don't think Susie went that way, but you're right." He lowered his voice, so only Roger could hear. "Make sure someone stays with Becky. I don't want her left alone, or the next thing you know, she'll be out looking for Susie."

The sheriff nodded. "I'll see to it that Mildred doesn't leave her side."

Jared started after Laurie at a jog. Though the sky was getting darker, the air hadn't cooled, and he wondered why people found jogging so invigorating. Running in a hundred-degree steam bath wasn't his idea of pleasure, especially not uphill. Swimming, on the other hand, was cool and refreshing.

He'd started swimming laps when the doctors recommended it for Joann; he hadn't wanted her swimming alone. Since her death, he'd continued his daily ritual of twenty laps. It was relaxing, mind cleansing. And it had beneficial side effects.

For a man pushing forty, he was in pretty good shape. No potbelly. No flabby muscles. He liked to think of his body as a lean, mean machine. Nevertheless by the time he reached Laurie, he was ready to slow to a walk.

And he coughed. Not continuously, as his father had begun doing ten years ago, but one deep, racking cough that made him glad he'd quit smoking when he did.

Laurie didn't stop or even look at him, but he saw her back stiffen and her head lift a bit higher. He supposed someone making noise while her dog was working was also unacceptable to her. However, he had questions he wanted answered. "How do you know your dog's following my niece and not someone else? Or something else, for that matter?"

She glanced at him then, her expression controlled. Only her eyes revealed her irritation. "How do I know? Because I work with this dog every day. I know that once he's given a scent, that's the only scent he'll follow until he finds what he's been asked to find."

If being president of a business didn't require him to question everything, he might have accepted her answer. Instead he challenged her. "A lot of time has gone by since Susie disappeared. That makes a difference, doesn't it?"

"Not that much time has gone by. If conditions are right, Cappie can follow a trail that's forty-eight hours old."

"So how are conditions?"

"Well, the high humidity and no wind are good, but this heat doesn't help, and her—" She shot him another glance, and her tone changed from objective to conciliatory. "We'll find her."

"The heat doesn't help, and . . . What else?"

"And . . . she's a child. Children don't leave a

strong scent. But trust me. I can tell by the way Cappie's working that he's on your niece's track."

The smile she gave him was totally unexpected, warm as sunshine and truly beguiling. *Trust her?* What choice did he have? It was follow her dog or check places he'd already checked.

One more question kept nagging him, and it had nothing to do with his niece. "How old are you, anyway?"

"Twenty-nine."

His brows rose in surprise.

"You don't look that old." He'd been thinking she was twenty-two at the most. There wasn't nearly the age difference between them that he'd imagined.

"Thanks . . . I think," she said dryly. She spared him another glance. "And how old are you?"

"Thirty-eight."

"Figures." Her gaze skipped from his face to his body. "You don't look that old either."

Touché, he thought. He supposed he deserved that. "Do you often work alone? Just you and your dog?"

"Not usually, but sometimes a call will come in—like today—where we're the closest team. To be honest, I wish we had more teams in this part of the state, and if I ever win the lottery and get rich, that's what I'd like to do: train search-and-rescue teams."

He shook his head. "That's not what I meant. When you're called to do a rescue, like today, is it common for just you and your dog to go out? Alone?" He wasn't sure how to phrase this. "As small as you are, shouldn't you always have—"

She didn't let him finish. Stopping, she whirled to face him, all pluck and verve. "Are all blue-eyed blonds male chauvinists, or am I just lucky? Look, no matter what you think, I don't need someone holding my hand. I'm not a little girl. I am of legal age and quite capable of taking care of myself."

With a toss of her head that sent her ponytail swishing across the gear bag on her back, she turned away and started walking again after her dog.

Jared knew he'd really put his foot in it that time. Maybe it was because he'd had to watch over his sister for so many years and then his wife, but he'd never thought being concerned for a woman's safety made him a chauvinist.

"I didn't mean you weren't capable," he said. "I meant, going off into these woods by yourself isn't safe, not even for me, and . . ." He decided he'd better leave it at that.

She didn't look at him. She just shook her head, as though she'd tolerate him, but that was all. "Usually when I'm on a search, someone from the police or sheriff's department goes along. That's for liability reasons as well as safety. And when I'm training, there's often another person along. I always used to get Ruth, my business partner, to help, but now that she's married, I've had to find others who are willing to play lost."

Lost, Jared repeated silently. The knot that had formed in his stomach the moment his sister first called twisted tighter. He watched the dog quarter back and forth ahead of them and sighed. "I wish we were playing a game today."

Laurie glanced at him, and once again the tone of her voice softened perceptibly. "Mr. North, I know this can't be easy for you. You really should go back."

His answer was firm. "I'm not going back."

"Two of a kind," she muttered, and walked on.

"What's that mean?"

"Nothing."

For a few minutes, except for the songs of the fox sparrows and evening grosbeaks, there was silence. Jared watched the shepherd zigzag across the field, the dog's head high as he sniffed the wind. Sometimes the dog stopped, retraced his path, then stopped again. That bothered Jared. "Why doesn't your dog put his nose down to the ground when he's smelling?"

"Cappie both wind-scents and tracks. There are advantages and disadvantages to both ways. Since your niece wouldn't have left a lot of scent on the ground, he's picking up traces of her from the air and grass."

"I don't know anything about dogs," he admitted.

She almost smiled. "I didn't think you did."

"I guess I don't know anything about children either." He looked at the trees ahead. Each step was drawing them closer to the woods. "I was sure Susie wouldn't be in there."

"You never know what children will do. Maybe we'll be lucky. Maybe your niece will be smart. Did any of you ever teach her about hugging a tree?"

"Hugging a tree?" He chuckled at the image. "It would have to be a small tree. Susie's not very big."

"The size of the tree doesn't matter. What's important is for the person who's lost to stop walking, sit down, and stay put. Believe me, it makes finding a person a lot easier."

A rumble of thunder caused both of them to pause and look toward the southwest. The storm was getting closer. On the horizon, like a strobe, flashes of heat lightning illuminated pewter-colored clouds. *Hug that tree, little Susie*, Jared silently prayed.

"Cappie seems to be having a little trouble following the scent," Laurie said. "I think we should split up. Keep about ten yards apart. That way we can check a wider area, see if there are any signs of your niece. I'll walk in this direction, and you go that way." She waved her hand toward his left. "Make sure you watch for snakes."

"You do the same." Both timber rattlers and cottonmouth moccasins were in the area, which made Susie's being lost all the more dangerous.

As Jared walked on, he angled toward the left, looking in the grass for anything out of the ordinary. What was truly extraordinary, though, he thought, was the woman he was with.

He watched Laurie swipe the back of her hand across her damp brow, never breaking stride and ever scanning the field. He had to admit he was impressed with the lady. She might be small in size, but she was all business, all energy.

And she was damned cute, the color of her hair a mixture of golden-brown and ginger, her skin a rosy pink that reminded him of the peaches that grew in southern Illinois, her small nose perfect for her face, and her mouth tempting. Under other circumstances he'd be attracted to her. As it was, he couldn't imagine why a woman this pretty and petite wanted to do this kind of work. It just didn't make sense.

Her ponytail bobbed enthusiastically with each step she took, and something about the rich color reminded him of a chestnut pony he'd once wanted as a boy. He'd pleaded with his parents for that pony, but he'd never gotten it. His father had considered animals poor investments.

Funny that he'd thought of that now.

Since his sister's call he'd done a lot of remembering back to when he was a boy. He'd tried to think of places he would have hidden. Considering the mischief he'd gotten into back then, he'd come up with a lot of possibilities. Nevertheless none of them had panned out.

Glancing down the hill toward the farmhouse, he noticed how far they'd traveled. Susie was an active child, yet it still seemed a long way for her to have wandered. He yelled over to Laurie, "Have you seen any signs of her?"

"No."

Neither had he. "You're sure your dog's tracking her?"

"Yes, Mr. North. I'm sure. Why are you so certain your niece wouldn't go into the woods?"

"Because we've told her not to."

Laurie laughed. "You're right, you don't know much about children. Telling them not to do something is like saying, 'Do it.'"

That might have been true with him, he admitted, but not Susie. "She's always been a good girl."

"We're not talking about good and bad, we're talking about kids and curiosity."

The Captain trotted off to the right and began sniffing in a circle, his head close to the ground. "I think he's found something," Laurie called, and immediately started toward her dog. "I'm going to check it out."

Jared was right on her heels. By the time he reached her, she had stopped by the edge of an area of trampled-down alfalfa and weeds. "Looks like the Captain found where some deer were laying up," she said.

The dog cast about the trampled grass, his tongue lolling out the side of his mouth and his panting audible. Jared felt as hot and thirsty as the dog looked, and mosquitoes and deer flies were beginning to bother him. Suddenly the trek up the hill seemed a big waste of time. "Looks like your Captain has taken us on a wild-goose chase." Irritation laced his words. "Or, more appropriately, a wild-deer chase."

Laurie gave him a measuring look. "Still questioning my dog's abilities?"

"I haven't seen anything to convince me Susie came this way." He knew he wasn't making points with the woman, but at the moment he didn't care. What he wanted was to find his niece.

The clouds racing overhead had grown darker. Air that had been deathly still only moments before now stirred with a breeze, and a turkey vulture soaring high above was rocked by down drafts.

The wind brought some relief from the heat, but not much. Mostly it brought the smell of rain. Jared knew the storm was coming faster than they'd expected. "Even if your dog was following Susie," he said, "he'll lose her once it starts raining."

"Not *if* he was following her, Mr. North. My dog *is* following your niece. And if it's not a heavy rain, it won't wash her scent away."

The mosquitoes and flies increased their attack on him. One buzzed near his ear, another got him on the back, and a third landed on his arm. He swatted at each and hoped Becky had put repellent on Susie before they went outside. He didn't want to think what the flies and mosquitoes would do to her tender skin. Or what would happen if she got into ticks.

"Here," Laurie said. "Put some of this on while I contact the sheriff."

He stared at her. She was holding a small bottle of insect repellent toward him. On the grass by her feet sat her open gear bag. Caught up in his thoughts about Susie, he hadn't even noticed Laurie removing the bag from her shoulders.

She smiled. "The way those flies are attacking you, you must be a tasty morsel."

"Considering what the flies usually go after in Tom's barn, that's not very flattering." He gladly took the bottle from her, surprised that he once again felt a tingle of warm vitality when his fingers brushed hers. "You do come prepared, don't you."

"In the summer, repellent is a basic for search-and-rescue work."

"I take it you've used it already." He'd noticed the flies and mosquitoes weren't bothering her nearly as much as they were him.

"I put some on back at the farm."

"What else do you have in there?" He nodded toward the bag as he applied the repellent to his arms.

"A bit of everything."

From what he could see, he believed her. In view was a first-aid kit, a knife, matches in a container, a water bottle, and two flares. Buried beneath those items was more. A lot more.

He watched as she removed the two-way radio from its case on her hip, her movements both graceful and efficient. Within seconds she was talking to Roger Olsen. As she detailed what they'd done and found, Jared unbuttoned his shirt and began rubbing the oily repellent on his chest, across his shoulders, and as far down his back as he could reach. Twisting and flexing, he tried to get every spot the flies were attacking and protect himself against a possible tick infestation. When he finished, and straightened, he caught Laurie staring at him.

Her gaze was focused on his bare chest, then it shot up to his face. Swiftly she turned away, but not before he saw her cheeks turn pink. How long she'd been staring at him Jared didn't know. He also didn't know why, but it pleased him.

Recapping the bottle, he dropped it back in her bag. "You find Susie, and I'll owe you one," he promised. Later, he added to himself, they could decide what he owed her.

"You don't owe—" she began, but the sheriff's voice coming over the radio interrupted her.

"The park rangers just drove into the yard," Roger said. "You going to wait for us? Over."

"I don't think so," Laurie answered. "Cappie's checking things out, and as late as it is, if he finds a track, I want to keep on it. Over."

"Checked things out," Jared corrected her. "Your dog just ran into the woods."

"No!" Laurie spun toward the trees. "Cappie, come!"

A roll of thunder drowned out her command.

"Laurie," Roger said, "storm's coming in too fast." He sounded rushed. "I'm calling off the search for now. You two get back down here immediately. Over."

Laurie looked at the sky, at the trees, then she faced Jared. "Look, you're a civilian. You shouldn't even be here. Go on back."

"Hey, if you say your dog's going to lead us to Susie, then I'm following your dog." No lightning storm was going to stop him from finding his niece. And he certainly wasn't hightailing it back to the farm if this pint-sized woman was gutsy enough to stay out.

Or maybe they were both idiots, he thought. Another flash of blue-white lightning connected land to sky, and a sharp, eardrum-splitting crack followed immediately. Jared gave an involuntary start, and so did Laurie.

Without thinking, he started to put his arms around her. Thunder-and-lightning storms always scared Joann. She'd said she felt secure in his arms and would nestle close until the storm passed. Laurie's reaction was just the opposite.

"What do you think you're doing?" she demanded, twisting away from him, her body rigid.

"I, ah . . . the lightning . . . I was just offering a little comfort," he stammered, feeling like a fool.

"Well, I am not a child. I don't need comforting during a lightning storm. Do you understand?"

Roger's call over the radio forestalled his answer. The sheriff's transmission was frantic and constantly breaking up. "I re . . . eat, Laurie. Jer. Return . . . farm!"

Laurie lifted the radio to her mouth. "We're going into the woods." She stuffed the radio back into its case and closed her gear bag.

Before she could lift it, Jared put his hands over hers. It was silly for her to carry a bag when he could do it far more easily. "I'll take that."

"No!" She tightened her hold on the straps. "I carry my own gear."

"I insist."

Her voice took on a steely edge. "No, *I* insist! And I'm the one who's in charge here, remember?"

A puddle-sized drop of rain hit her upturned face right on the top of her nose. It would have been funny under other circumstances. Then another hit her cheek, and one got him on his forehead, and he knew the storm had arrived. They didn't have time for a battle of wills.

He lifted his hands, and Laurie picked up her bag and slipped it over her shoulders. She ran up the hill like a gazelle, heading for the safety of the woods. He was the lion following her, catching up to her, measuring his strides to match hers.

Rain turned to hail, striking with icy sharpness, spurring them on to greater speed. "Where did Cappie go in?" she yelled.

"I'm not sure. There's a path—an old road—to our right." It was the one Tom and he always took when they hiked up to the rocks. Jared veered to the right, certain she'd follow.

They entered the woods running. The dense pines immediately blocked out the hail and most of the day's remaining light. The wide path in front of them became a shadowed course of fallen branches and stones. Jared stumbled, caught his balance, and stopped.

Laurie had stopped a few feet behind him and was leaning forward, hands on her knees. She was sucking in deep breaths of air, and the rapid rise and fall of her chest worried him.

Walking back to her, he touched her shoulders. Immediately she straightened and looked up at him.

"Are you all right?" he asked, concerned. Joann had often had trouble catching her breath.

"Fine."

"You're sure?" His fingers quickly found the pulse at her throat. It was rapid and strong, not faint as Joann's had usually been, and for a moment he knew what it would be like to touch a hummingbird.

But only for a moment.

Slapping his hand away, Laurie glared at him. "I said I was fine. Look, Mr. North, I think we need to get some things straight here. You don't need to pamper me. I can take care of myself. In fact I'm the one in charge. You follow me, not the other way around. That includes deciding where we go. Do you understand?"

"I was just trying to help." Her determination to be in charge was beginning to irk him. He'd seen the dog go in. He knew where the path was. It was logical for him to take the lead.

"You want to help?" she asked through clenched teeth. "Stay out of my way."

She dropped her bag from her shoulders and began digging through its contents. In moments she had what she was looking for—a flashlight. She snapped it on and cast its beam over the ground, then reached back into the bag and pulled out a second flashlight. This one she held up to Jared. "Here, for now you can use Cappie's."

"Your dog uses a flashlight?" A faint chuckle rumbled in his chest. "Does he carry it in his mouth or in his paws?"

"Very funny. I fasten the light to his harness. So I can see him."

"Where is your dog, anyway?"

"He'll be checking back in."

Slowly she cast the beam of light over the trees. Weather roughened trunks absorbed the light, while the hail that penetrated the canopy of leaves turned into sparkling gems. Captured, warmed, and filtered, the moisture became a gentle sprinkle that pattered soothingly to the ground, cleansing the air and intensifying the smell of pine and decaying foliage.

When her light hit the dirt by their feet, the only prints Jared saw were deer tracks. Crisp V's. Dozens of them.

As he'd guessed, the damn dog was chasing deer. They'd hiked up a hay field and were now stuck in the woods, while who knew where Susie was. Not here, he was certain. Susie wouldn't have come this far, wouldn't have gone against her father's orders. Jared had hoped the dog could find her. Now the animal was off chasing deer, and he didn't know what to do.

Automatically he reached into his pocket for a pack of cigarettes, then remembered he'd quit. Frustrated, he pulled out a piece of gum. Even that was his last. It had been a rough evening.

Laurie walked forward, following the trail, her light focused on the ground. Jared took only a few steps after her. Each showed exactly the same thing—deer tracks.

"Just how far do you intend to walk this trail?" he asked, not bothering to disguise his frustration.

"A way farther."

"I suppose I could build a fire. I saw you had matches. At least we could dry out some while we wait for this storm to blow over and your dog to come back." The temperature had plunged at least fifteen degrees in the last ten minutes, and under the trees it felt even cooler.

"I wouldn't get too settled yet."

"Why?" If she were looking for a job, he'd have hired her solely for her perseverance. She literally left no stone unturned, or at least no branch. He watched her pick up a recently fallen pine bough and toss it to the side. "What are you looking for?"

Turning, she smiled and beckoned. "Come here."

He obeyed, the light from his flashlight mingling with hers as he reached her.

"Look," she said.

An area of soft dirt by her feet showed the distinct print of a dog's paw. That really didn't surprise him. "So? We know your dog came this way."

"Now, look over here." She moved the beam of light to the left, closer to the edge of the path, where she'd lifted the pine bough.

For a moment Jared simply stared. There in the dirt was the clear imprint of a child's tennis shoe. "So she did come this way!"

He knew he sounded surprised. He could also tell from Laurie's smug smile that she was enjoying his surprise. "Come now, Mr. North," she said, lightly teasing him, "don't tell me you had doubts?"

He grimaced. "You know I did. Erroneous doubts, it seems."

"Glad to hear you admit that." She stood, brushing the loose dirt from her hands. "Now, let's just hope your niece didn't wander too far into these woods."

He held the same hope. "Up ahead is a section of limestone rock formations that are really treacherous." Tom had taken him there several times. The difficult climb was worth it, for the view of the valley below was impressive. "The area's not as picturesque as the Garden of the Gods, but it's just as dangerous." And he remembered that a girl had slipped and fallen from one of the rocks in the Garden of the Gods. She'd ventured too near an edge and was now a quadriplegic.

"Don't go imagining the worst," Laurie said.

He didn't want to, yet it was hard not to be realistic. He watched as Laurie hurried back to her gear bag. Quickly she zipped it closed.

"I don't suppose you'd let me carry that for you now?" he asked.

Her no was immediate.

"Or lead the way? I do know those woods better than you."

"Which really doesn't matter, does it?" She waved her flashlight over the ground. "It's your niece's trail we're following, and the only one who knows if she stayed on the trail or not is Cappie."

"Who's not here."

"He'll be back."

Laurie led the way, moving slowly, always checking the path for signs of her dog's paw prints or impressions of a little girl's tennis shoes.

Jared soon decided she was right, it was better for him to follow. As the last vestiges of light disappeared, it was nearly impossible to see beyond the range of their flashlights. From behind her, though, he was in a position to see over her head yet guard her flank.

The storm was nearly directly above them, and the hail had changed to a steady rain. Thunder rolled across the sky like a bowling ball down an alley, while the lightning cracked and snapped like a bullwhip. With the wind whistling through the treetops, it was difficult to hear much of anything, but over and over Jared called Susie's name, hoping against hope she'd answer.

She didn't.

He hated the thought of her being lost in the

woods, alone in the dark. Alone during a storm. The kid had to be scared out of her wits. Even to him the boulders and trees had begun to take on ominous shapes.

Laurie continuously angled her light from side to side, fanning it across the tree trunks and bushes, rocks and dirt. Jared kept his pointed straight ahead, and he stiffened when he saw something moving. It was on the trail, far down the path. Something dark. Something running toward them, fast.

He reached out and put a hand on Laurie's shoulder. "I think you'd better get behind me."

Three

Laurie halted but stood where she was. "Why?"

"Because there's—"

He stopped abruptly, feeling foolish when he realized what he'd seen was her dog. The Captain was trotting toward them, a stick hanging out of his mouth, his tail wagging like a wet sable banner. He stopped in front of Laurie and dropped the stick.

She held it up for Jared to see. "This means he's found your niece."

It was just a piece of wood, part of a branch. Nevertheless he stared at it as though it bore a message from heaven. "Where is she? Is she all right?"

"I don't know. All he's been trained to do is bring back a stick when he finds what he's looking for." She hugged and praised her dog, then stood. "I'll need your light now."

He gave her the flashlight, and she strapped it to the dog's harness. She gave one soft command, and the Captain turned and headed back in the direction he'd just come, moving at a slow trot.

The trail grew steeper and more rugged, and the pines and cedars thinned to a sparse few trees. The multihued sandstone formations for which the Shawnee National Forest was renowned loomed all around them, the rocks pushed up from the earth's interior millions of years before, then molded and eroded through eons of climate changes. In daylight the huge rock bluffs were magnificent to view and fun to climb. In the dark they were simply dangerous.

Above their heads heavy, opaque clouds emptied themselves, while cracks of lightning, incredibly close, split the sky. Jared felt the hair on the back of his neck stand up. Being out in a storm like this was crazy—stupid—but the Captain was traveling unhesitatingly, climbing up the staircased cliff, the flashlight on his harness a bobbing beacon of his progress. And Laurie was right on the dog's heels.

Out in the open. Heading for Susie.

There was no time for common sense.

"Watch your step," Laurie yelled, never slowing as she scrambled and clawed her way up the slope.

He was more concerned about her steps, as each took them higher. Rivulets of rainwater followed long-carved gashes in the rock, spilling over the sides like small waterfalls. Lichens covered the sandstone, making the surface slick. One misstep, one mistake, could take either of them over the edge.

Gusts of wind close to forty miles an hour didn't help. "Do you want me to hold on to you?" he shouted, still worried about her slight build.

The wind blew away part of her answer, but he gathered it was the same as usual: She wasn't a child.

"Then be careful," he told her.

He couldn't see the Captain ahead of them, but was sure they were still following him. On this bluff there was little the dog could do but climb upward. Jared simply hoped that when they reached the top, they'd find Susie.

All right.

Alive.

A crack of lightning hit unnervingly close, the sound and the light simultaneous. Laurie started, jerking away from the rock, then gasped. Jared knew instantly that she'd lost her footing.

Almost in slow motion, her flashlight flew up into the air, then down. Her hands reached out, wet fingers finding only empty air. One foot no longer touched rock, and her body tipped to the side.

She was going over the edge.

He moved without thinking, grabbing whatever parts of her he could reach. One hand wrapped around her ankle, the other clamped down on the pack of her back. He held on and swung his body in the opposite direction, back against the rocky bluff.

If she'd weighed more, she might have taken them both over. As it was, Jared had no trouble keeping her from slipping any farther, and she quickly found a hold, then her footing.

But he didn't let her go. Pulling her to him, he held her close, his heart in his throat and the adrenaline pumping. And for the first time since they'd met, Laurie Crawford didn't object to something he'd done. She simply lay against him, breathing hard.

He still felt shaky when she slowly pulled away and inched her body toward the edge. Cautiously he crept behind her, and together they looked down. Far below lay the flashlight she'd carried only moments before, its resilient beam still shining, illuminating a section of rocks. Laurie expelled a deep breath, then turned and touched his arm. "Thanks."

"Don't mention it."

She didn't after that. Getting back on her feet, she started off again, scrambling ever higher.

He noticed, though, that she now hugged the inside of the trail. She also didn't say anything when the walkway narrowed and he grabbed hold of her pack to give her added support until the path widened again. At the top of the bluff the Captain trotted back to her, nudged her hand, then moved on again, leading them over and around mounds of rocks.

The rain continued to drench their clothing, while the wind chilled their skin. Jared used the flashes of lightning to scan the area, but he almost missed the sandstone cave. And when he first saw the huddled shape inside the opening, he wasn't really sure what it was. Only the long silvery-blond hair caught his eye.

"Susie?" he called, but her name was drowned out by a roll of thunder.

The dog headed straight for the form, and another flash of lightning gave Jared a better look. It was Susie, her knees drawn to her chin and her face hidden under an arm. As she lifted her elbow and peeked out, he saw the fear in her wide blue eyes.

Immediately he slipped around Laurie and ran, his shoes sliding on the wet rocks as he scrambled past the dog. "Susie!" he cried, and ducked under the protective cover of the cave's roof. Dropping to his knees, he enfolded the child in a protective embrace. "Oh, Susie. Are you all right?"

"Uncle Jer! You came!" Her sigh said it all. Small hands clung to him, hugged him, and a petal-soft mouth kissed his cheek. "I couldn't find the way home. I saw a baby deer in the field and tried to catch it, but it ran away. I know I wasn't supposed to come here, but—"

"But you're all right?" That was all he cared about. Later Becky and Tom could deal with what she'd done. He just wanted to hold her, assure himself she was alive and well.

"I'm fine. I thought if I climbed up these rocks, I could see where my house was." She sniffled and hiccupped. "But it started rainin', then little white rocks started hittin' me, so I came here."

"Smart girl." He wiped away the tears stinging his own eyes.

Laurie knelt beside them. "She's all right, then?"

"Seems to be."

"I'm kinda hungry," Susie admitted.

"Well, then we'll have to find you something to eat, won't we," Laurie said. "Then we'll let your mommy know we've found you."

Slipping off her gear bag and digging deep, Laurie came up with a packet of granola bars and a container of juice. "Here's something you can work on."

Susie released her stranglehold on Jared and took the packages Laurie offered. The juice she gave to him to hold; the granola-bar package she eagerly tore at. "Is it a cookie?"

"Not really a cookie. It's sort of like cereal all crunched together."

"Oh." Susie paused for a moment, then continued to tear open the package.

As Susie crammed the crumbly oat bar into her mouth and washed it down with the juice, Laurie attempted to get in touch with the sheriff, and Jared checked his niece for cuts and bruises. Susie was dirty and had a few insect bites and scratches on her legs and arms, but her shorts and top were nearly dry. The only ill effect of her adventure seemed to be hunger. She'd finished one granola bar and was working on a second when Laurie held the radio toward her. "Your mommy wants to talk to you. You'll have to talk loudly, the transmission is still fuzzy."

Gone was the frightened child. Sitting close to

Jared, Susie held the radio next to her mouth and rapidly retold her story to her mother. "I thought a big black bear with a funny collar was gonna get me, but he's just a dog. He brought Uncle Jer and a lady I don't know to find me."

Susie absently patted the Captain's head while she talked. By the time Laurie finished her last transmission and put her radio away, the dog was lying in a corner of the cave with Susie curled up beside him. The child stroked the Captain's shoulder, her blond hair mingling with his sable coat. Snuggled against the dog's soft, warm side, she closed her eyes.

"She's exhausted," Jared whispered, sitting by his niece. "I suppose I should get her up. In another minute she's going to be asleep."

"Let her sleep," Laurie said. "I know from experience Cappie makes a great pillow, and you heard what the sheriff said about another storm being right on the tail of this one. Until that lightning is over, I'm not going out on those rocks again."

He agreed. They'd been lucky. As high as they were and with no protection, they'd been walking targets for the lightning. And the cave his niece had discovered wasn't bad. Though not big, probably no more than eight feet from front to back and maybe twelve feet wide, nature had formed a fairly spacious shelter for them. He would have to either crawl or walk stooped over to move about, but Laurie could stand up straight, he noted.

To dig into her bag, however, she knelt. "I have some space blankets in here," she said. "I want to put one over Susie, and—" Crawling close to Jared, she stole the flashlight from her dog's harness. "I need this more than he does right now."

The beam of light passed over Jared, and she stopped to look at him. "Thanks again for catching me, Mr. North. That was a real heart stopper."

"Glad to be of help." He smiled. "And don't you think it's time we were on a first-name basis. It's Jared."

"Okay . . . Jared." She smiled, too, first at him, then down at Susie. "It's always a good feeling when you find them safe and sound. I was worried about her."

"So was I."

She moved back to her gear bag and shone the light into it. "Here. This is what we need."

What she held up for him to see was a small packet, which very quickly became a wide, light-weight, aluminum-coated, insulated sheet. She unfolded it completely and laid it over Susie. "That will keep her warm."

The child slept on, not even stirring, while the dog simply sighed. Laurie gave him a loving pat. "You did a good job, boy."

Back at her bag, she again dug around, occasionally using the flashlight to check out an item. "I know I have more of those blankets in here. When the sheriff called, I decided to travel light and just take the blankets. I even went and got two more. So where are they?"

Leaving Susie's side, Jared crawled closer to Laurie. She vigorously pushed things from one side of her bag to the other, then began pulling each item out until she had a pile by her leg. As he'd thought, she had just about everything except the kitchen sink in there—maps and paper in a plastic bag, sunscreen, rope, extra batteries. There were sacks that he assumed held food and toiletries, and even a camera and binoculars.

While she continued to rummage through the contents, he checked her left hand. She wasn't wearing a ring, but that didn't necessarily mean she wasn't married. He wanted to know. "What's your husband think of you doing this search-and-rescue work?"

"It's ex-husband, and he thinks I'm crazy."

"Boyfriend?"

She stopped her rampage through her bag and looked up.

"Fiancé? Steady? Significant other?" Jared went on. "What's he think of you being out in weather like this, going into the forest at night and climbing steep rocks?"

Her expression serious, Laurie sat back on her heels. "Well, first of all, if any guy objected to my search-and-rescue work, he wouldn't be a boyfriend, fiancé, or significant other. And second, lately I haven't had time to go out on a date, much less develop a relationship."

"I'm a widower." Not that she'd asked, but he wanted her to know. "My wife died five years ago."

"I'm sorry." She shook her head. "This is like déjà vu."

"I don't understand."

"You—" She stopped herself and smiled. "You remind me of someone I know."

She returned to her search through her gear bag. Studying her, he mused that she certainly didn't remind him of anyone he knew. "I can tell by your accent that you're not originally from around here. How long have you lived in Norton?"

"My accent?" She laughed. "I don't have an accent. I don't drawl my words out and talk slow. It's you guys who do—you, and Ruth, and the sheriff, and everyone else down here. Around Chicago people talk the way I do."

So she'd come from the Chicago area. That was a start, but he wanted to know more. "How'd you come to move down here and get involved with search-and-rescue work?"

"He got me involved." She pointed toward her dog. "When I bought him, he was just a puppy, and a real little hellion. I knew he needed some obedience training, and when I started asking around about a place to take him, I found out a neighbor not only gave obedience lessons, but was a member of a search-and-rescue team. I talked to Jim, he gave me a book about search-dog training, then let me help with one of his training sessions. After that I was hooked. And you know the rest of the story."

He didn't, but he wanted to. "You told my sister that you own a pet shop. It's here in Norton?"

"Yes. LaRu's. I take it you haven't heard of it." She sounded disappointed. "Actually I co-own it, with Ruth Banning. Thus the name LaRu. La for . . ." She waved a hand in the air. "Well, you know what I mean.

"Ruth's name used to be Ruth Youngs. She grew up here in Norton, but was living and working in Chicago when I met her. Actually she was dating Jim when we met. Sometimes Ruth would help with the dog training, so I got to know her pretty well.

"After Ruth and Jim broke up, she and I would still get together for lunch or dinner at least once a month. She didn't really like life in the big city and was planning on moving back here, so when I started having trouble with my ex, she suggested we go into business together and open a pet shop in Norton. Which we did, two years ago." Laurie held out a granola-bar packet. "Want one?"

"No, thanks. What kind of trouble were you having with your ex-husband?"

"Not terrible. He just has this idea I'll come back to him." She sat cross-legged and opened the packet. "You'll have to excuse me. All I had for lunch was an apple and I missed dinner. I'm starved."

He loved the enthusiasm she showed as she attacked the oat bar. She seemed to attack everything with enthusiasm. "So, will you go back to him?"

"To Greg?" Her brows drew together in a frown as she let her gaze rove from his face to his shoulders, then back to his face. Finally she shook her head. "No. I've put that part of my life behind me. I like it here. Norton's just the right size town for me, not too small and not too large. I only wish the pet shop were making more money."

"I didn't even know about your place." Without thinking, he leaned close and brushed a crumb from the edge of her mouth. Something about sharing the drama and fear of the search for Susie with her, as well as sitting so close to her in the small cave with rain falling outside, inspired a strange sense of intimacy in him. Touching her seemed perfectly natural.

Her breath caught, and her gaze locked with his, and he smiled. "I owe you a dinner," he said softly. "For you missing yours tonight." He let the backs of his fingers travel over her cheek. Her skin was still damp from the rain, but velvety soft. "I know a nice place in Harrisburg." A quiet, romantic restaurant where they could talk, have a few drinks, get to know each other. "How's Friday night sound?"

She let her breath out with a small shudder. "Friday night?"

Abruptly she pulled back, away from the touch of his hand. Looking down at her bag, she shook her head. "No, it just wouldn't work."

"All right, Saturday night, then."

"No." She didn't look at him. "I—I just can't. I'm . . . ah, too busy."

"Forget Harrisburg, then." They could do that another night. "We can go somewhere in Norton. Get just a quick bite." Any time with her would be better than none.

"I really can't."

She said it tersely and kept her eyes averted.

That puzzled him. He reached over and put a hand on her arm. "Look at me, Laurie."

She did, slowly.

"What's the matter?"

He felt her shiver, and her voice was shaky. "It wouldn't be a good idea for me to go out with you."

"Why?"

"Well, for one thing, you see me as small and helpless."

"When I first met you, yes. Now I see you as small, pretty, and dedicated to what you're doing. I also see you as a lady I'd like to get to know better."

"You're always trying to take over."

"No, I—" He grinned. She was probably right. "You can blame that on my job. I run a company of two hundred employees. I'm used to being in command."

"My point exactly."

Never before had a woman told him she didn't like him because he was a CEO. "All right, then," he said, willing to compromise. "You set the date and place we have dinner."

"You don't understand. It's not when or where. It's . . ." Again she shook her head. "I just can't go out with you. It wouldn't be a good idea."

He could feel the goose bumps on her skin. Gently he stroked her arm. "You're cold."

Her laugh was tight and nervous. "Crazy, isn't it. An hour ago I was too hot, now I'm too cold."

He touched her sleeve. "Your clothes are soaked."

"Yours are too. If there was some dry wood around, we could start a fire."

They both looked out of the cave. What few sticks and branches were lying on the rocks were soaked. She began digging through her bag again. "Those space blankets should be in here. They'll keep us warm. I remember putting them on the table next to my bag, then . . ."

He watched as she pulled the last few items out of her bag and knew exactly when she gave up looking for the other insulated sheets. She gave a mild curse and mumbled something about leaving her head behind if it weren't attached. He grinned. Maybe she didn't have those space blankets, but there was more than one way to stay warm. Leaning forward, he encircled her waist with his hands and pulled her to him.

Light as a snowflake, she plopped into his lap. She sat where she'd landed for a second, and he marveled at how right she felt. Then she moved suddenly, twisting to get up, and he had to tighten his hold to keep her from getting away. "Laurie, don't get up. I just want to help you get warm."

"I don't need your help," she insisted, wiggling vigorously.

He hadn't thought about what would happen once he was holding her . . . once her hips rubbed against his. The more she squirmed, the more his body responded. His intention had been to help warm her, but he was the one getting hot. And aroused.

Reluctantly he let her go.

She stood quickly, turning away from him. "Why did you do that?"

"Because you're cold. I wanted to help warm you."

"I don't need help. I'm not a child, Greg. I can do things on my own."

"My name's not Greg."

She whirled and faced him, staring wide-eyed, her lips slightly parted. "Oh, dear, I'm sorry," she apologized, and laughed, though not convincingly. "I don't know what's wrong with me tonight. I just . . ." A deep breath of air seemed to clear her head, and she straightened. "I don't like to be grabbed like that."

"Okay, maybe I shouldn't have grabbed you. I'm

sorry about that. But I do know two bodies touching generate more warmth than one. You're cold. I'm cold. We don't have wood for a fire. You don't have any more insulated sheets. Cuddling together only makes sense."

She didn't respond, and he figured it hadn't helped that he'd gotten an erection the moment her cute little tush landed on his groin. "I'm not going to try anything," he added, "if that's what you're worried about. My motives are honorable." Or at least, he admitted silently, they were in part. "I just want to take care of you."

That wasn't the right thing to say, for she bristled immediately. "I don't need taking care of."

Her reaction surprised and irritated him. Hell, all he wanted was to help . . . and maybe enjoy the pleasure of holding her for a while. It had been a long time since he'd held a woman in his arms.

Standing—or more accurately, stooping—he faced her. "Okay, maybe you're fine, but I'm not. I'm wet and cold, and I'm going over there"—he pointed to the back of the cave, not far from where Susie and the Captain slept—"where there's less wind. If you want to join me, fine. If not, fine. It's your decision."

He found as comfortable a place as he could and settled back against the wall. He hadn't been kidding, he was cold. His shirt and trousers were soaked, and his shoes felt like sponges. Wrapping his arms around his knees, he watched Laurie.

She stood where he'd left her, staring out at the rain. The wind blew a fine mist of water into the front of the cave, and the torrent from the sky showed no signs of relenting. Finally she glanced over her shoulder, first looking at Susie, then at him. When she began putting her thing back in the bag and when she slipped on the plastic raincoat she'd had in there, he was sure she was stubbornly going to maintain her defensive attitude. But once she'd zipped her bag shut, she turned off her flashlight and walked back to where he sat.

Even she had to lean over as she neared him. "I decided you're right," she said. "We can help keep each other warm." Clearing a spot, she sat down beside him. "I'd let you use this raincoat, but I don't think it would go around your shoulders."

"Don't worry about it." He wouldn't have taken it from her even if it had fit. Besides, simply having her close instantly increased his internal thermostat.

Her shoulder touched his arm, and he breathed in deeply, inhaling her sweet, feminine smell. She was rainwater clean, and he caught the lingering scent of a flowery shampoo, a hint of repellent, and an aroma that was uniquely herself.

Flashes of lightning continued to illuminate the sky and allowed him to study her profile. She'd closed her eyes, and whenever the lightning hit close, she'd flinch, but he didn't think she was afraid. It was more a reaction to the sound than fear. He'd goofed when he'd tried to comfort her in the field. He had a lot to learn about this woman.

She spoke first, her voice soft. "I heard Jesse James and his gang used to ride all around this area and hide out in caves like this."

He chuckled. "If Jesse James did all the riding and visiting that people around here say he did, he wouldn't have had time to rob banks. But who knows, maybe he and Frank sat out a storm in here, just as we are."

A shiver shook his body, and she looked at him. "You are cold, aren't you?"

"I'll live."

She snuggled closer and slipped an arm around his waist. "How's that?"

It was nice, but he had a better idea. "Uh . . . could you maybe sit on my lap? Sort of block the wind? I mean, with you having the raincoat . . ."

He was surprised when she climbed on his lap without a protest. He'd expected a caustic laugh and a refusal. For a few minutes he didn't move or say a thing, his thoughts concentrated on keeping his lower body relaxed. He didn't want to scare her off again. But when she rested her head on his shoulder, he couldn't resist pushing a wet strand of hair back behind her ear.

She tensed, then relaxed. "I must look a mess. I'd just hopped out of a shower when the sheriff called."

"You look fine." Gently he stroked a lingering raindrop from her cheek.

"You getting warmer?" she asked.

"Yes." His temperature was soaring. "How about you?"

"Much warmer."

Her voice was shaky, and he snuggled her closer. "You know, whoever said big surprises come in small packages must have been talking about you. You really impressed me this evening. I'd like to get to know you better."

"I . . . it wouldn't work."

"That's what you keep saying, but how do you know? If you want references, I'll get them for you. I think most people consider me a nice guy. Other than a few beers on the weekends and an occasional cocktail now and then, I don't drink. I've now gone six weeks without a cigarette. I don't gamble, at least nothing more than a small wager on a football or golf game. And I don't play around. In fact I haven't been out on a date in months."

"Jared, really, you don't need to tell me all this."

"Maybe not, but it's either talk to you or kiss you."

She sucked in a quick breath. "Maybe you'd better talk."

He would have preferred the other choice, but

took her suggestion. "I did do a lot of dating right after my wife died. I think I was trying to find what I'd just lost, but I guess I'm what you'd call a one-woman man. Joann was more than a lover. When she died, I lost a good friend."

"What a nice thing to say."

"That's what I keep trying to tell you. I'm a nice guy."

"I liked the way you treated your niece," she admitted, shifting position on his lap and getting more comfortable.

"Susie's a sweet kid." Jared prayed for strength. He'd thought he'd lost his sex urge—it certainly hadn't bothered him for the last few months—but being around Laurie was having a powerful effect on his libido. "I do have one problem."

"What's that?"

"Talking didn't help. I still want to kiss you."

It took her a moment to answer, and when she did, her voice was husky. "I really don't think that's a good idea."

"Why?" Despite her plastic raincoat, the way she was leaning against him, he could feel her breasts. Her nipples were hard. Maybe it was because of the cold, but he wanted to think it was because he was affecting her the same way she was affecting him.

"It would be foolish," she said.

"You sure?" She might be protesting, but she was also rubbing his arm, running her fingertips over his biceps in a gentle caress.

"It's crazy. The way you act." Her voice was faintly breathless. "The way you look . . ." Her hand slid seductively over his chest. "Everything about you. I told myself I'd never again get involved with a man like you."

"And what kind of a man am I?" He lowered his mouth to hers.

She whispered her answer.

Four

"Domineering and possessive." That was what Laurie said.

Jared didn't know about domineering, but she might be right about him being possessive, because he wanted nothing more than to possess her mouth. He could feel her breath warm his chin, her fingers knead his arm. Her lips were a hair's breadth away. Much too close to resist.

In the dark his kiss didn't land exactly on her mouth, but that didn't matter. What did matter was she didn't pull back, didn't resist. Instead she clung to his arm, tipped her head to the side, and brought their lips into perfect alignment.

She'd said she didn't want to get involved with him, yet her mouth immediately turned soft and responsive, and her lips moved over his with the guileless passion of a woman who cared. No, she wasn't a passive bystander. He wasn't even certain if he was kissing her or if she was kissing him.

And he didn't care. It was enough that the chemistry working on him was working on Laurie too.

Only when she shifted her weight, rubbing her bottom across his lap, did he wonder if they weren't both playing with fire. He was achingly aroused. Where was the stoic control he normally had around women? Maybe it was the cave. He felt lustfully primitive, proud to be a male, and ready to take her then and there.

Cradling her head in his hands, he breathed her name, cherishing it, savoring it. He'd found wonder, excitement. Boldly he thrust his tongue into her mouth.

If she had pulled away, he wouldn't have stopped her—it wasn't his nature to force a woman—but she opened to him, taking him in, letting her tongue play with his. She tasted like sugar and spice . . . like the first sip of Dom Pérignon. He was getting heady and heard himself groan. Or was it she? Everything they did seemed to be synchronized. Her hands traveled up to his neck and laced through his wet hair, even as he loosened her ponytail. His fingers combed rain-soaked tresses, discovering their thick and silky texture. Their tongues parried, and when he wrapped his arms around her, she hugged him tight.

Jared wanted more, yet it was all too new—her taste, her feel. Nothing about Laurie had followed his expectations. She certainly wasn't helpless. Nor childlike. She was Dresden china and tempered steel. Innocence and unabashed need. Warmth. Life.

For the first time in years he wanted to rejoin the living.

Gasping for breath, he drew back to look at her. The thunder and lightning had moved on, and in the darkness he could barely make out her face. Still, he knew she was staring up at him with the same wonder he felt, that her heart beat was as rapid and erratic as his. Being cold was no longer a problem. He was on fire, inflamed with a need that was unsettling.

Laurie was the first to speak, shakily. "We . . . I shouldn't be—"

He pressed a finger to her lips. Maybe they shouldn't be clinging to each other, he thought, kissing and arousing desires that couldn't be satisfied, but it seemed so right. "Stay," was all he said.

She exhaled an unsteady breath, but complied, and after a minute he felt her relax. Leaning against him, she rested her head on his shoulder.

The rain came down steadily and hard, and the wind continued to blow, but within the cave Jared heard only little sounds—Laurie's sigh, the crackle of her raincoat, her intake of breath and its slow release.

When she placed her small hand flat against his chest, he wondered if she had any idea how good it felt. Or if she realized how erotic the light touch of her finger tracing his collarbone could be. Slowly she ran her hand over his arm, pressing his wet shirt to his skin. He was in heaven.

He was in agony.

He'd turned into a horny old man, his need embarrassingly evident and certainly not something he could satisfy, even if Laurie were willing. Not when his niece was sleeping only a few feet away. Not when he wasn't prepared.

She continued to stroke his arm, and his muscles flexed automatically. She murmured her appreciation. "What do you do, lift weights?"

"I swim. Every day."

Delicately she traced the outline of his biceps. "Why is it I'm attracted to blue-eyed blonds with great bodies?"

"Are you?"

"I seem to be."

"Maybe you just have good taste." He kissed her forehead. "Actually you taste a little like mosquito repellent."

"But you're not repelled?"

"Nope." Entranced was more what he felt.

The radio on Laurie's hip emitted a crackling noise, then they heard the sheriff's voice. "Laurie, you there?"

Her sigh said she was no more ready for the intrusion than Jared was. Roger Olsen had to call twice before she answered.

The sheriff's message was short and to the point. The second storm was going south of them. The rangers were on their way, would be there within minutes. Their time alone was coming to an end.

Jared knew it didn't really matter. This night was just the beginning. Laurie and he would have tomorrow, and the next day, and every day after that to get to know each other.

"How can she not be there?" Jared shouted into the telephone. "Look, you tell her she can't keep hiding, that if she won't talk to me on the phone, I'll show up on her doorstep."

The answer he received wasn't what he wanted to hear. Irritated beyond reason, he slammed down the phone. Maybe he shouldn't take his frustration out on a woman he'd never met, but damn, he was tired of getting the runaround.

While Laurie and he were in the cave, everything had seemed so perfect. Then the rangers had come, and the moment one shined his flashlight on Laurie's face, Jared knew it was obvious she'd been kissed. He hadn't thought what the stubble of a day's growth of beard would do to her delicate skin. Or how his mouth would bruise hers. Her cheeks were too pink, her lips too puffy.

So, he'd joked with the rangers about not having enough blankets to stay warm and having to improvise. The men had grinned.

He hadn't expected Laurie to get all huffy.

Then there was the bit with her gear bag. Picking up the bag and carrying it back to the farm had been a natural response for him. He'd known she had to be tired. Besides, it had been easier for him to walk with Susie balanced on one hip and her gear bag slung over the opposite shoulder.

Yet Laurie had glared at him as though he'd committed a travesty, sparks practically flying out of those big brown eyes of hers. As soon as they were back at the farm, she'd snatched her bag from him and stalked straight to her car.

He'd taken Susie to Becky. His sister had cried and laughed and hugged her little girl, and Jared had hurried back outside to talk to Laurie. But in the few minutes he was inside, she'd packed up and left. Dog and woman were gone, without even a good-bye.

He hadn't seen her since. Not for a week and a half.

It hadn't helped that most of that time he'd been out of town—in Springfield, Omaha, and Boise, attending an unexpected series of meetings with the president and vice-presidents of Arp Industries.

His only contact with Laurie had been two frustrating telephone calls, his first on Wednesday, the day after they found Susie. He'd called her that morning at the pet shop, right after he thought she'd have opened. He'd wanted to tell her he'd be out of town for a while and to set up a dinner date for when he got back. He hadn't had a chance to mention dinner. She'd spared him no mercy, burning the lines with her tirade, telling him exactly how obnoxious his behavior had been and where he could go.

It wasn't out on a date with her.

The second time he actually talked to her was on her home phone. Two rings and her answering machine clicked on. He was halfway into his message when she picked up the receiver. She was fuming, and he didn't get more than five words out before she demanded he never call again and hung up.

Not that he didn't call her after that. Two or three times a day—from every city and every hotel he stayed in—he called, dialing either the pet shop or her home. He left messages with her partner, Ruth, and on her machine; told her he was sorry, that he'd never meant to embarrass or upset her; and left numbers where he could be reached. He even gave her his calling card number, so that she could call him free of charge. He sent her a written apology, too, along with a check. The money, he told her, was in appreciation for the wonderful job she and her dog had done in finding his niece. He wanted her to realize he did respect her abilities.

But she never called.

Now that he was back in Norton, Ruth had changed her excuse and simply said Laurie wasn't in.

Frustrated, Jared rose from his desk and went to his window. Looking at the gleaming blue-and-silver buildings that housed the design division and manufacturing plant of North Machinery usually filled him with a sense of pride and satisfaction. Today though, nothing eased his distress, not even the satisfaction of knowing a week and a half of intense negotiations had resulted in a signed contract that would make both the stockholders and his employees very happy. Times might be tough for some companies, but North Machinery wouldn't be laying off people for a long time to come.

Now was the time to celebrate.

Only the woman he wanted to celebrate with wouldn't even talk to him.

He burst out of his office and stopped directly in front of his secretary's desk. "Am I bossy?"

Grace Kelser had been with the company for nearly two decades, first as Jared's father's secretary and now as Jared's private secretary. She was pushing fifty, but her dark skin showed few lines, and her mind was as quick as her tongue. Looking up from the letter she was typing, she diplomatically turned his question around. "You are the boss."

"That's not what I mean. Am I a bossy man? Do I order people—you—around?"

Her dark eyes twinkled, and her wide smile showed straight white teeth. "At times. You are like your father in a lot of ways."

That wasn't what he wanted to hear, but he knew Grace was being honest. If anything, the woman treated him more like a son than an employer. "So you're saying I am bossy?"

"I'm saying you're the boss. Bosses give orders. You, in my opinion, do it very nicely. Much more nicely than your father ever did. Now, honey, what is the problem?"

"The problem is one pint-sized female who won't talk to me because she says I'm too bossy."

"Then stop bossing her around."

"All I did was try to help her out a little. Is it my fault I was raised to be a gentleman?"

Grace gave him one of her I-want-to-know-more looks. "What's her name?"

"Laurie Crawford. She's the one with the tracking dog. The one who found Susie."

"Ahh." Immediately Grace began thumbing through a stack of mail on the edge of her desk. "Maybe things aren't so bad after all. That name was on a letter you received today. On the return address." She found the letter at the bottom of the stack. "I didn't open it." She winked. "It's marked 'personal.'"

"Thank you." He took the letter and stared at it for a moment, then walked back into his office.

He felt like a teenager. Simply holding a letter from Laurie made breathing difficult. His heart was hammering harder than an extrude press, and his hand actually shook when he used his letter opener.

Why had she written? To accept his apology? To apologize herself for being so curt?

It turned out to be neither. In the envelope was his check and a piece of paper. She'd returned the check he'd sent in appreciation for finding Susie and written a brief note. Actually it was a very formal thank-you for the check and an explanation that she didn't accept payment for what she did. If he wanted to express his appreciation, he could do so by making a donation to NASAR, the National Search and Rescue organization. She'd finished with, "Sincerely, Laurie Crawford."

Sincerely.

The way she'd responded to his kisses had been more than "sincerely." She had kissed him. That night she'd been as much a participant as he'd been. Now she was trying to act as though nothing had happened.

Well, dammit, he thought, something had happened. It had hit him like a kick in the gut, but he'd found a woman he wanted to get to know, in all aspects of the word. And he wasn't going to sit around and let her brush him off like a bit of lint.

Crumpling the check and note into a ball, he tossed them into his wastebasket, then grabbed his coat and headed for the door. He was going to do what he should have done as soon as he got back in town.

Jared knew the address for LaRu's Pet Shop from when he'd mailed the check to Laurie. Nevertheless it took him a while to find the place. It wasn't situated in the downtown business section of Norton, but in an area zoned both residential and commercial. The shop was attached to the side of a one-story, World War I vintage home. Both house and business had the same white aluminum siding, green roof, and green shutters. What distinguished one part from the other was the large red-and-white sign above the door to the pet shop and a spacious gravel lot.

Two cars were parked there, a fairly new gray Chevy and a blue Ford Escort, which looked like it had seen more than a few years and miles. Recognizing the Ford as Laurie's, he pulled his white Cadillac El Dorado up next to it, but he didn't get out. Laurie worked and lived here, and he had no idea what to do next.

An open-air flower booth at the end of the street gave him an idea. Five minutes later he entered the pet shop carrying a bouquet. He would have preferred roses to daisies and zinnias, but the booth owner's offerings were limited. And the colorful flowers did look bright and cheerful, which was what he wanted.

It was a peace offering, though he truly didn't know what he'd done wrong.

There were no customers in the shop, and he saw Laurie right away, toward the back, by the fish tanks. She was talking to a tall, lanky blonde who was wearing a blue jumpsuit and an apron. Both women looked his way as soon as the bell on the door tinkled its warning. The blonde smiled and nodded; Laurie's eyes widened and her lips parted, but she said nothing.

He walked directly toward them, his gaze on Laurie. She was even prettier than he'd remembered, and, oddly, more petite. In a blue miniskirt, blue-and-white-striped blouse, and white sandals, and with her hair down and curling loosely around her face, makeup enhancing her large brown eyes and accenting her sweet mouth, she looked like a Barbie doll.

"Must be my lucky day," he said. "Seems you are in, after all." He did spare the lanky blonde a glance. Considering the lack of anyone else in the shop, she had to be the one he'd talked to on the phone so many times. Laurie's partner, Ruth. The one who always said Laurie was busy—or out.

"Mr. North," Laurie said. "What a surprise." She nervously licked her lips, moistening them and making them even more alluring, though he doubted that was her intention.

Ruth let her gaze move slowly up and down his body. Her look was appreciative, and she smiled when she turned to Laurie. "He called again, about twenty minutes ago. Said he was coming over. I told him not to. I didn't think he would."

"I got tired of hearing you were busy . . . or out," he said. "Oh, and you'd better have your answering machine checked. I left several messages. Evidently you never got any."

Laurie lifted her chin and squared her shoulders. "There was no need for me to call you. We've discussed everything that needed to be discussed."

"No, you told me I was an insensitive cad who could go fly a kite. That's not a discussion."

Actually he didn't want to discuss anything. He wanted to reach out and take her in his arms. Hold her tight. Kiss her until she stopped pushing him away and would listen to him.

What he did was hold out the flowers. "These are for you."

"I don't want gifts either." She turned away and began straightening cans of fish food.

"Laurie, we need to talk."

Keeping her back to him, methodically moving cans from one spot to another, she shook her head.

"Are you afraid to?"

That stalled her hand and turned her head. "No, of course not."

"Then just give me a few minutes." He glanced at Ruth, then back at Laurie. "Alone."

Again Laurie shook her head. "It's not a good time. Ruth and I were talking."

As far as Jared could see, they could do that at any time. He turned to Ruth. "I ask you, is it fair for a woman to decide something won't work without giving it a chance?"

"Oh, no, you don't," Ruth said, lifting her hands in supplication. "Leave me out of this. Laurie makes up her own mind."

"And I know all I need to know," Laurie said. "Ruth, you are looking at Mr. Take Charge. Give him ten minutes and he'd probably reorganize our pet shop."

Jared wasn't interested in reorganizing her business. It was Laurie herself he wanted. "You're being unfair. I let you take charge Tuesday," he reminded her.

"*Let me!*" Her voice rose a notch, and she lifted her chin dramatically. "You didn't have the right to let me or not let me. And you didn't have to point out to those rangers that I'd gone and left those extra space blankets on the table. You made it sound like I was crawling all over you."

"I never said you were crawling all over me. I said you'd thought you had extra blankets but you couldn't find them, so we found ways to stay warm. I was trying to make light of something that was very obvious."

"Well, I didn't consider it funny."

The way Ruth was grinning, she evidently did. Laurie noticed and glared at her partner.

The entry bell tinkled behind Jared, and Laurie's gaze darted to the door. "I need help," a strident female voice announced.

Jared turned as two women came into the shop, one of them carrying a small white poodle under her arm. She smiled a broad, cheeky smile. "Fifi and I are going to go to obedience school. I need a special collar and leash."

"I'll help her," Ruth said, and winked at Jared. "That should give you your chance to talk to Laurie. Privately."

"Thank you." He'd seen a door behind the counter and was sure it led to the house. "Can we go in there?"

"Why not?" She finally did take the flowers from his hand. "Might as well put these in water. I hate to see living things go to waste."

Her rigid posture as she led the way into her house said his stopping by was a waste—a waste of his time. Nevertheless he wasn't about to give up, not until he was absolutely sure he didn't have a chance. He wasn't a quitter.

The moment he stepped into her house, he grinned. It looked as though it had been hit by a tornado.

"You'll have to excuse the mess," she said, laying the flowers on a newspaper spread across her kitchen table. "I was on a search last night and most of this morning."

"So, you were gone."

"Since just before midnight. An old man over in Cairo wandered off from a convalescent home. Cappie and I went, along with two teams from up north. We started at daybreak, and he was found around ten. Not by us, though. The police picked him up in Springfield. The old man had hitched a ride there the night before, then just wandered around until someone noticed him." She pushed a chair over to the refrigerator, then climbed up and opened the cupboard above it.

"Can I help?" he asked, though he found watching her stretch for a glass vase far more pleasurable. Her blouse tightened across her breasts, clearly delineating firm, nicely rounded curves, and her skirt rose high on her thighs.

"I've got it," she said.

As she turned to get down, he stepped close and wrapped his hands around her waist. Easily he lifted her to the floor, holding her so her legs touched his, then her hips. The feel of her body was an aphrodisiac, and the look in her eyes told him she wasn't as cool and indifferent to him as she'd like him to think. Immediately, though, that look turned to a glare.

"I said, I had it!" Twisting out of his grasp, she walked to the sink.

She had to clear away several dirty dishes before she found room to fill the vase with water, and she kept her back to him all the time, but he could tell she was upset. He was beginning to doubt the wisdom of coming. He wasn't doing anything right.

"I received your note today," he said. "And the check."

She said nothing, and for a moment he wondered if she'd heard him over the sound of the running water. Then she shut the water off and asked, "So if you got my note, why did you come?"

"Because I had to. Laurie, what happened between us that night, it meant something to me."

She looked at him. For a moment her expressive eyes showed the same hunger he felt, then she turned back to the flowers. Her answer was given with a sigh. "You wasted your time in coming here. What happened between us that night . . . Well, I can't explain it, but it would be absolutely ridiculous for me to go out with you."

"Why?"

The telephone hanging on the kitchen wall rang before she answered. She glanced at it, but didn't move. Again it rang.

Tension tautened her mouth, and her gaze never left the telephone. After the second ring her answering machine clicked on. Jared knew the recorded message by heart. It said to call the pet shop during the day, especially if it was a rescue call. Otherwise leave a message.

Finally a male voice came over the line. "Laurie, pick up the phone. It's Peter."

The tension immediately left her face. She picked up the telephone as she turned off the machine and spoke softly into the receiver.

Jared knew it was wrong, but he purposely eavesdropped, catching the gist of the conversation. Peter had called the pet shop and had been told Laurie was in the house. Peter had been with her on the search for the old man. She laughed and told him yes, she'd tried to get a little sleep, but no she hadn't.

Pure, unadulterated jealousy twisted through Jared.

Had she been in bed with Peter earlier? Had he left her to go home, to let her get some sleep, only to miss her so much, he'd called?

To tell her what? That he loved her?

To hear her say she loved him?

She looked disappointed, but it wasn't words of love she murmured. "I understand," she said. "No, that's all right. If your wife needs you there, she needs you there. I'll try to find someone else to lay track tomorrow, otherwise I'll do that exercise another day. See you Tuesday night?"

She waited for an answer, and Jared held his breath, still afraid he'd hear her voice quaver.

Her response was level. "Oh, I see. Well, that's too bad."

She sighed when she hung up.

"Problems?" he asked.

"Another one bites the dust." Her laugh held no mirth.

"The wife didn't want to share him?"

"That about sums it up."

He wondered at her casualness over the ended affair. "So now?"

"I keep trying, I guess."

"I'm available," he reminded her.

"I thought you said you didn't have a dog."

That totally confused him. "I don't."

"Then how could you train one?"

He began to understand. "This Peter was training a dog?"

"Every Tuesday night and on the weekends. He has a really nice Lab that would make a great search-and-rescue dog, and he's really interested in doing it, but his wife is jealous of me. Which is absolutely silly." She returned to the flowers. With frustrated anger she thrust them into the vase.

Jared could understand the wife's fears. What man wouldn't want Laurie? "You are very pretty."

She seemed surprised by the idea, then shrugged. "My looks shouldn't have anything to do with this. I'm not after her husband, and he isn't interested in me. All he wants is to train his dog, and all I want is to help him so he can pass the tests. Plus, he was helping me. I was going to put Cappie through a SAREX—search-and-rescue exercise simulating a real mission—tomorrow. Now . . ." Again she shrugged.

"I'll work with you."

"You'll what?"

If Laurie wouldn't go out with him, he decided, then he'd go out with her. She didn't think he respected her abilities. He'd show her he did. "I said, I'll work with you tomorrow. I'll lay track or whatever you need done."

"Don't be ridiculous."

He smiled. The more he thought about the idea, the better it sounded. "What time tomorrow?"

"This isn't a game."

"I know it isn't. I'm quite serious. You need someone to help you with a training exercise, and I'm offering. What time?" he repeated.

She smiled, smugly. "Five o'clock . . . in the morning."

He knew she was hoping he'd back down, change his mind, or come up with an excuse why the time was too early. He wasn't about to give her that satisfaction. "I'll be here."

Five

It was dark at five A.M., and the air was pleasantly cool, though the weathermen were predicting clear skies and temperature in the eighties later that day. Jared had barely slept the night before and was up before his alarm went off. Laurie had told him to wear boots and clothes he wouldn't mind getting dirty. An old pair of tan golf slacks and a green-and-white-striped Polo shirt seemed his best choices for the clothes. He'd had to buy the boots, though.

When he arrived at her house and she looked him over, her gaze traveling slowly from the stripes on his chest to the unscuffed toes of his boots, he watched her expression. She was frowning. "Why, in heaven's name, did you wear new boots?" she asked.

"Because I don't own any old ones."

She shook her head. "This isn't going to work. An hour after you start, you're going to have blisters the size of quarters."

He knew she was looking for excuses, any reason to cancel and get out of spending the morning with him. He wasn't about to let her. "My feet will be fine. The shoe salesman said these boots break in fast. Are you ready or not?"

She continued looking at him, and he could almost follow her thought process by the direction her gaze took. It dropped back down to his boots, and she shrugged, obviously accepting that he wasn't going to back out. Then she looked up, directly at his mouth. Abruptly, she turned away. "I'm ready."

She was again wearing the khaki slacks, blouse, and orange vest. He noted that her hiking boots were definitely scuffed and well broken in. Moving quickly, she picked up her orange gear bag and a clipboard with a printed form, grabbed a leash and an orange collar, gave the Captain a pat and a "Let's go," and turned off the lights in her house.

"We'll take my car," she said. It wasn't a suggestion but an order, and she headed for the blue Escort.

Laurie and her dog moved with the efficiency of a team that had lived and worked together for years. Jared felt distinctly like an outsider.

It bothered him that she could so totally ignore him, when simply being near her had his generator racing. She methodically went about her business, storing her bag in the trunk of the car, letting her dog into the backseat, pulling her keys from her pockets.

Jared watched every move she made, and when she started whistling he realized she was ignoring him too much, trying too hard to act casual.

"So, where are we headed?" he asked as he settled into the passenger's seat and buckled his seat belt.

"Stonefort." She turned to look over her shoulder before backing onto the street. For just a moment her eyes met his. She looked away quickly.

Much too quickly.

He reached over and looped a finger through the armhole of her vest, purposefully letting his knuckles rub close to her breast. "Do I get a vest too?"

He felt her suck in a breath just before he pulled his finger away. She wouldn't look at him, but the way she gripped the steering wheel, he knew she wasn't ignoring him anymore.

"You're going to be the victim," she said, her voice huskier than it had been. "Victims don't wear vests."

"Sounds reasonable. I've been a victim ever since I met you."

She stepped on the brake, jerking them to a stop, and finally looked at him. "Jared, this isn't going to work."

"Why not?"

"Because . . ." She didn't seem to know what to say. "Because . . ."

He knew why. Because for some reason she was afraid to get involved with him. Because she wanted to pretend he was just someone there to help her. Because she wanted to forget that she'd ever kissed him. Only he wasn't going to let that happen.

He wanted her to remember back to that kiss and to go on from there, for her to be aware of him, to react to his touch, to get a little breathless and flushed every time he was near.

He wanted her to want him as much as he wanted her.

"It will work," he assured her. Satisfied he'd ended her pretense of indifference, he leaned back against the seat. "Now, tell me what I'm to do."

"You're serious about this?"

"I'm serious."

She hesitated a moment longer, then shifted and turned onto the street. Heading toward State

Highway 45, she explained what they'd be doing. He listened, the administrator side of him appreciating the thoroughness with which she gave her instructions, while the purely male side of him loved the way she pursed her lips when she was thinking, loved the lyrical sound of her voice and the light, flowery scent that surrounded her.

She was enthusiastic about the exercise. He couldn't say he felt the same. Basically what she wanted was for him to get lost.

It seemed like she'd been telling him to do that since they'd met, but this time there was a practical reason for her demand. She wanted to practice for a proficiency test, and he was to be a moving victim. He'd have an hour's head start, and the Captain's job—along with Laurie—was to find him.

Jared's hopes of spending the morning with her were gone, at least until she did find him. Once they arrived at their destination, they'd be separated for two or more hours, and he wasn't looking forward to that.

She was still talking when he reached over and touched her hair. It was as soft and silky as he remembered, and she'd tied it back again, this time with a scarf. It was too dark still to see her clearly, but her slender, graceful neck made a nice silhouette. Without thinking, he pressed his fingertips against the side of her neck. Her pulse was strong.

"Why do you do that?"

Her question made him pull his hand back.

"When we were looking for your niece," she added, "you took my pulse then too."

"Habit, I guess."

"You take everyone's pulse?"

That did sound ridiculous. "No, but I often took my wife's. She had a weak heart, but she never wanted to be a burden. There were times she'd push herself too hard if I didn't keep a check on her."

"I'm strong and healthy."

"I know." Again he pressed his fingertips to her pulse point. This time he smiled. "You do have a rapid pulse."

"I always get excited before an exercise."

He let his fingers slid up to her cheek. Her skin felt warm, flushed. "We have a lot in common. I get excited before certain kinds of exercise too."

"Jared, don't." She brushed his hand away. "You're distracting me."

"Good." That was exactly what he wanted to do. He let his gaze roam over her body. "Did I tell you, you look lovely this morning?"

"I'm not supposed to look lovely. I'm supposed to look physically fit and capable. Besides, how can you tell what I look like? It's dark out."

"I saw you when you answered the door. You look physically fit, capable, and lovely."

"I think you'd better study the map in the glove compartment." She was changing the subject, but there was a breathless quality to her demand. "Turn on the overhead light and familiarize yourself with the section I've marked. I'd like you to follow the railroad tracks for a while. I want to see what effect, if any, that has on Cappie's ability to track you. And if there's a place where you can cross water, do. Only watch out for moccasins. They give me the creeps."

He had no desire to meet up with one himself.

She continued listing her requests. "Cross fields. Go into the woods. Do anything you can to hide your trail."

"And what if I succeed?" He did want her to find him.

"Cappie will have failed the test." She laughed, lightly and teasingly, and Jared wondered if she'd purposefully fail to find him.

Maybe she realized he was worried, because her tone quickly turned serious. "Don't worry, I'll give you a compass and you'll have that map. Around here there's a road every mile or so and farmhouses you could go to. But don't unless it's absolutely necessary. At O-eight hundred I want you to pick a spot and stop. Hopefully Cappie will find you before nine, since I'd like to be back at the shop by ten. But if I haven't found you by eleven, you should head back to the car."

"Did I happen to mention," he asked, "how bad I am at reading a compass? My folks constantly sent me to summer camps, but I always flunked the survival tests. I could be wandering around looking for your car for hours."

"Oh, great."

"So you'd better find me."

The moment Laurie turned off the car's ignition, the Captain was on his feet, whining excitedly. She patted him on the head and told him it would be a while. As though he understood, the dog lay back down.

Getting out of the car, Jared stretched and looked around. Stonefort, like so many small towns nestled in the Shawnee National Forest, was a mixture of businesses and homes surrounded by sprawling farms and dense woods. Tilled fields abruptly changed to managed timber; flat bottom land ran up against hills untouched by glacier. Rivers, streams, and creeks crisscrossed the area, accounting for its nickname of the Illinois Ozarks. Farther to the west were large lakes, where Jared's grandfather had taken him fishing when he was a boy.

Laurie had driven beyond Stonefort and down an unpaved road, stopping by an open field. He could see one farmhouse in the distance. A quarter moon hovered above the hills, and the first glow of dawn lent an eerie atmosphere to the landscape. From the farmhouse a dog barked, its lonely cry sending a shiver down Jared's spine. *He'd been reading too many Stephen King novels lately,* he thought, *it was getting so his imagination ran rampant in the dark.*

"You may need a flashlight for a while," Laurie said, and pulled her gear bag from the trunk of the car. In a minute she had a flashlight out for him.

He took it and snapped it on, casting the beam over the field. He was glad it would be light soon. The footing wasn't going to be that level.

"And here's some food," she said, "just some granola bars to snack on, and a canteen of water. I filled two this morning." She handed one to him, keeping the other for herself.

"Mosquito repellent," she added. "And Sevin. Dust it on your pant legs and around your belt to keep the ticks off."

"Lovely thought." He took the can and began dusting his pants.

"First-aid kit." She set it on the roof of the car. "It includes what you would need for a snake bite."

"You're all full of good news." He dusted the Sevin around his waist, then set the can down.

"Better prepared than sorry," she said. "Here's a canvas bag you can use to carry everything. You can tie it to your belt or sling it over your shoulder, whichever is more comfortable." She checked her bag again. "Anything else you can think of that you'd like?"

"A kiss." He'd been thinking of it since he'd first seen her that morning. He wanted to hold her in his arms, to absorb her vitality.

"Forget it." She laughed nervously and quickly zipped up her bag, using it like a barrier between them. Even in the dim lighting, though, he could tell her cheeks had reddened, and when she did glance his way, her eyes revealed conflicting emotions.

The idea of sharing a kiss excited her, he could tell, yet she was retreating from the possibility. He could have forced one on her, and maybe she would have responded, but he didn't want to take that chance. For some reason she was certain getting to know him would be bad. It was up to him to prove she was wrong.

"In that case . . ." he said, and took another look at the map. "Stonefort's that way?" He aimed his light back the direction they'd come.

"That's right."

"And you want me to get lost in there." He flashed the beam on the woods on the opposite side of the field.

She nodded, and he swallowed back his sigh. There were dozens of things he'd like to be doing with Laurie. Walking away from her into a forest infested with insects, snakes, and vermin wasn't one of them. Still, he'd promised . . . damn his impulsive tongue. "Okay," he said. "See you around."

He did reach out and brush the back of his hand across her cheek. He wanted just one touch, a memory to carry with him. "You be careful now, you hear. Don't go talking to strangers, and all that good advice."

With as roguish a smile as he could muster, he turned and started to walk off.

"Wait!" she called after him.

He heard the yearning in that one word. The need. She didn't want him to go any more than he wanted to leave. She wanted him near her, touching more than her cheek. Making love to her.

Beaming with satisfaction, he spun back around.

"I need something of yours for Cappie to scent on."

His euphoria died with a strangled chuckle. What *he* needed was a psychiatrist, he told himself. Since meeting this woman, his mind had been totally messed up. Maybe a two-hour walk in the woods would do him good, get his head back on straight.

"Here." From his back pocket he pulled out his wallet.

"You're sure?"

"It's that or the shirt off my back."

"Okay." She pulled a plastic bag from her gear bag and held it open so that he could drop in the wallet.

He checked his watch. "It's almost six." And already nearly light, thank heavens. "Anything else?"

"No." Before he was two steps from her side, though, she added, "You be careful too. This is just an exercise, Jared. Don't do anything foolish."

He'd already done the foolish part, he thought. He'd gotten emotionally involved with a woman who had him totally confused. "I'll be careful," he answered.

How did a man prove he wasn't bossy, domineering, or possessive to a woman who'd already made up her mind that he was? Jared leisurely strolled along the railroad tracks, pondering that question. Far above him a hawk soared through the pale blue sky, while off to the side, in the woods, squirrels chirped and chattered, warning any who would listen of the presence of man. Deerflies circled his head, but he only occasionally swiped at them.

It was difficult for him to imagine anyone bossing Laurie around for long. She might be small in size, but everything he'd seen indicated she was a strong-willed person who took charge and directed her own destiny.

Possessiveness, however, was something he

could understand. What man wouldn't want to possess that woman? She was a treasure to be adored, a gem to be cherished. Her smiles were like the first rays of sunshine, warm and golden. Her laughter was a summer's breeze.

And even after eleven days and nights, he still remembered her kisses. They had sent reason to the farthest regions of his mind. Otherwise, why would a thirty-eight-year-old man, whose only love of hiking was to walk eighteen holes of golf, offer to get lost in the woods? Why would a man who wanted nothing more than to hold Laurie in his arms have walked away from her?

He had to be crazy.

At the sound of water he checked the map, guessed where he was, and left the railroad tracks to find the stream. By the time he reached its banks, the sun had cleared the tops of the trees and was warming his face. He followed the stream for a way, found a place to cross, then took a road that went into the woods. Only it wasn't a road, and suddenly it ended. Rather than retrace his steps, he went on. That was a mistake. By eight o'clock he realized he was no longer pretending to be lost. He was lost.

Looking at the map didn't help. Neither did the compass. So what if he could tell where magnetic north was? That wasn't going to show him where he was now.

He stuck the compass back in his pants pocket and searched for a stick of gum or a piece of candy. He wanted something to chew on, but a granola bar didn't sound good, which meant he was getting better. The first week after he'd stopped smoking, he'd eaten everything in sight. It was amazing he hadn't gained twenty pounds. Now he only occasionally felt the urge for a cigarette, mainly when he was frustrated—or lost—and a stick of gum or piece of candy usually satisfied the craving.

His search turned up two hard candies . . . and one cigarette. It had to have been in his pocket for months. Its paper was yellowed, the end was frayed, and some of the tobacco was missing. Overall it looked disgusting.

Slowing turning it between his fingers, Jared wondered how a man could become so dependent on something like a cigarette. He blamed his habit on his father. He couldn't remember a time when his father didn't smoke, which was why George North now wheezed when he talked, had had to retire early, and now lived in Arizona.

The fear of ending up with lungs that were just as bad had finally forced Jared to call it quits. Nevertheless he couldn't quite bring himself to toss the cigarette in his hand. Slipping it back into his pocket, he gave it a pat, then unwrapped one of the candies.

A recently fallen cottonwood lay by the trail, its branches still covered with green leaves. Jared checked it out, made sure there were no ant hills, termites, or snakes around, then picked as comfortable a spot as he could find and sat.

His boots came off right away, and two red spots on his heels proved Laurie's prediction to be more accurate than the shoe salesman's. The blisters weren't bad, but they needed tending. From the first-aid kit she'd given him he took two Band-Aids and covered the sore spots, then put his socks and boots back on.

Above and around him red-winged blackbirds sang their territorial songs, while crickets made music with their legs. A fly buzzed his head, then flew away. The sun warmed his body, and a somnolent lassitude closed his eyes.

• • •

He couldn't believe it when he looked up and saw Laurie coming toward him. She was smiling—no, laughing softly, sweetly. Her arms were open, reaching for him, and not a stitch of clothing covered her body. The sun shimmered off her long, free-flowing hair and bathed her skin with golden hues. Rose-red nipples accented full, firm breasts that gently bounced with each step she took. Only she wasn't walking, she was floating. Through the air. She was coming to him, opening herself to him.

"Jared," she called softly.

"Yes," he whispered, shifting his hips. He was hard and painfully ready for her. It was wrong that she had no clothes on and he was still wearing his. Wrong and strange, as was the lethargy that weighted his limbs.

The warmth of the sun was blocked from his face, then he felt her kiss.

Her wet, slobbery kiss.

Jared's eyes snapped open.

Up close was the black muzzle of the Captain, the dog's tongue hanging out the side of his mouth. Beyond him was Laurie—wearing clothes, her hair pulled back with a scarf, just as he'd left her.

He'd been dreaming.

Quickly he moved his hand to cover his crotch, then wished he hadn't. The movement brought her gaze to that part of his anatomy, and there was no way she could mistake the bulge beneath his fly for anything but what it was.

Chagrined, he smiled and patted the dog on its head. "So, I've been rescued."

"It took me longer than I'd thought it would," she said. "You did a good job. The way you wandered

around, especially at the end, was just like someone who's lost would do."

Jared saw no reason to admit that toward the
end, he had been lost. Pushing himself to his feet,
he stretched, then brushed the dirt from his
slacks, readjusting their fit.

He caught Laurie watching him. She quickly
looked away and picked up a stick. "Come
on, Cappie. You did a good job, boy. Time to
play."

The Captain barked and went bounding after
the stick.

"I reward him by playing a game of catch with
him whenever he makes a find," she said without
looking at Jared. "Give me a few minutes, then
we'll head back."

"No problem." He needed a few minutes to relax.
Not that watching her play catch with her dog did
much to ease the pressure in his groin. Every time
she pulled her arm back to toss the stick, her shirt
and vest tightened across her breasts. Maybe she
wasn't naked, but he did have a good imagination.
And when she stooped to retrieve the stick after
the Captain brought it back, he liked the way her
slacks hugged her bottom. He also liked it when
she glanced his way, then tried to pretend she
hadn't.

"Ever teach him any tricks?" he asked. "Like roll
over or play dead?"

"He knows all of the basic obedience commands—
he has to to be certified for search-and-rescue
work—but otherwise I don't have time to teach
him tricks. When he was a puppy I did work
on a couple. One was to shake hands, the
other was to take a cigarette out of a person's
mouth."

"That I'd like to see."

"The handshake?"

"No, your dog taking a cigarette out of someone's mouth."

"Actually I never got him so he'd do it right. He kept knocking me down. And that was when he was still a puppy." The Captain trotted back to her side and dropped the stick at her feet. "Good boy." She patted his head.

"What I wanted," she continued, "was to be able to say 'Smoking is a nasty habit' and have him gently jump up and remove the cigarette from the person's mouth before it was lit. What I got were more bruises on my rear end than I needed."

Jared's gaze dropped to her bottom, and he smiled. "I take it you're against smoking."

"You're looking at a reformed smoker. We're the worst kind of people to be around." She tossed the stick one more time, but the Captain didn't go after it. The dog's gaze was on her face, his tail dusting the ground behind him. "What do you want, boy?"

Cappie whined and held up a paw.

"To shake? Well, okay." She knelt and shook the dog's paw, then wrapped her arms around his thick neck.

It was easy for Jared to see that the relationship between Laurie and the Captain was more than that of owner and pet. There was a rapport he wished he shared with Laurie. He wasn't a man to beg and whine like a dog, but any time she wanted to hug him, he'd be happy.

"Ready to head back?" she asked, looking up at the sky. The sun was now high above them.

"I guess so." At least the trip back to the car would be with Laurie, he thought. He was banking on this time together to change her opinion of him.

Digging into his pocket for his last hard candy, he once again found the cigarette. He pulled it out, debating whether to strip it and toss it, or pack it home. He didn't have a chance to decide.

Although he saw the Captain spring up and start toward him, Jared still wasn't ready when the dog's feet hit his chest.

Six

"Jared, please, open your eyes. Talk to me."

He preferred listening—to the concern in her voice, to its slightly hysterical pitch. And feeling. Her hand wasn't smooth—no, it was the hand of a woman accustomed to doing manual work—but her touch was heavenly. Maybe it sounded like a groan, but he was purring when her fingers grazed his cheek, then his forehead.

"Please be okay," she begged.

Rocks were jabbing into his back, and his head felt like it had been used as a kick ball, but he'd live. He raised his eyelids slowly. Nevertheless the brightness of the morning sun forced him to blink several times before Laurie's face came into focus.

Hers was a beautiful face. The face of an angel. The face of a seductress. And he was more than willing to be seduced. Or to do a little seducing. "Hi," he said huskily.

She sighed. "Thank goodness. I'm so sorry. I don't know what made him do that."

A hairy black head suddenly blocked Laurie's face from view. With a snuff, the Captain poked his muzzle close, then started licking. Jared grimaced. That wasn't what he wanted. Twice in less than an hour he'd had that dog's wet tongue on his cheek. Both times he'd been hoping for a kiss from Laurie.

Raising an arm, he covered his face.

"Back, Cappie." Her command was softly spoken but firm. The dog moved away, though not without a whine of protest.

"He's worried about you," she said. "He didn't mean to knock you down."

Jared wasn't sure. She knew dogs; he didn't. But the way the Captain was watching him, wagging his tail, it was easy to imagine the black beast had enjoyed taking him off his feet.

Laurie gently touched the back of his head, and his thoughts left her dog. How tempting to groan and play the wounded warrior, he mused.

"How's your head feel?"

He did groan, but it had nothing to do with the tender spot she'd found. She'd leaned closer, so close that all he needed to do was lift his head and his lips would come into contact with her orange vest . . . with the V of tanned skin exposed by her shirt's open collar . . . with the hint of cleavage between her breasts. She smelled of sunshine and fresh air, mosquito repellent, baby powder, and femininity. It was a lethal combination.

His body reacted immediately, and he smiled. It was getting so that he was perpetually aroused when he was around Laurie. Any concerns he'd had about his age decreasing his sex drive were gone. Now he had to concentrate on keeping it under control.

She sat back and held up two fingers. "How many do you see?"

"Two."

She lifted another. "Now?"

"Three. And two beautiful eyes, one cute little nose, two tempting lips, one lovely neck, two—"

"Jared, be serious. Do you feel nauseated? Any numbness in your arms or legs?"

"I am being serious." He pushed himself up to a sitting position. As nice as it was having her worried about him, he wasn't comfortable playing the patient. "I'm fine."

He would have stood, but she placed a hand on his shoulder. "Do you feel dizzy?"

"No." Foolish and horny better described his feelings.

"Let me get a cold pack out of my gear bag."

He caught her wrist before she moved away. "Laurie, I have a little bump on the head, that's all." He could feel her pulse against his fingertips. It was as rapid as a trapped bird's. "Your heart's racing again."

"I'm concerned about you." Her voice had a breathless quality. "You were knocked out."

Gently he caressed her wrist with his thumb. "I wasn't out for long, was I?"

"No. Maybe a minute or two. It just seemed like an eternity."

"I've got a tough skull. I'll live." Actually, other than a slight headache and the tightness in his groin, he felt no different than usual. Even the tightness in the groin was becoming normal, at least whenever he was around Laurie. "Want to kiss and make it all better?"

She pulled her hand free and stood. "You're right. You're as crazy as before."

Jared got to his feet a little more slowly. Whether he wanted to admit it or not, being knocked down by a hundred-pound dog had shaken him. And he had hit his head on something. He warily touched the tender area and flinched. Laurie was watching him, her eyes laced with concern—and perhaps something else.

Desire, he hoped.

"Maybe we should sit for a while," she said.

She was treating him like an invalid. His pride wouldn't allow that. "No, I'm fine. Really. You wanted to get back to your shop before ten. Let's get started."

After a few minutes of walking, Jared wished he hadn't been quite so cavalier. Not only did his head ache, but the Band-Aids on his blisters weren't helping as much as he'd hoped. The one good thing was that Laurie had said the car wasn't far.

She'd taken the lead, which was a relief. Even before being knocked on the head, he'd had no idea which direction would take them back to their starting point. He'd been surprised when she headed to the right. Evidently he'd been traveling in circles for some time.

As they walked along the trail, she kept looking over her shoulder, checking on him. He knew she was still concerned that he might have a concussion. He also knew she could tell he was limping. At least she had the decency not to say "I told you so" about his boots. Actually she said very little until the trail was wide enough for them to walk side by side.

"I thought you told me you'd quit smoking," she said.

"I have."

"Then why did you pull out that cigarette?"

"I'd found it in my pocket earlier. I was going to toss it." Which, now that he thought about it, he guessed the dog had done for him.

"I shouldn't have taught Cappie that stupid trick. I never meant for him to go around knocking people down. You could have been seriously injured."

"He definitely caught me by surprise. Does he do that every time someone pulls out a cigarette?"

She looked at her dog. "He's never done it before.

I mean, not without me saying, 'Smoking is a nasty habit.'"

The Captain barked, spun around in front of Jared, and sat on his haunches. Every muscle in the dog's body was alert and tensed.

"Oh, my," Laurie gasped in understanding. "I said the words, and he took it as a command."

The Captain continued whining, watching. "No!" Laurie ordered. "No."

"See, nothing in my hands." Jared held his palms open in front of the dog. He was also prepared to pull his hands back and step aside, just in case the Captain mistook a finger for a cigarette.

"Heel." Laurie slapped her thigh and walked on.

For a moment the dog's gaze remained riveted on Jared, then years of training took over, and the Captain fell in beside her. Jared sighed with relief and followed.

"I never should have taught him that," Laurie said again, keeping close watch on her dog. "Blame it on Greg."

"Your ex-husband?"

"Yes. I was tried of him showing up at my apartment and polluting the place with cigarette smoke." She waited for Jared to come up alongside her. "I quit the day I left Greg. Now I can't stand the smell of cigarettes."

"How long have you been divorced?"

"It was final and official six years ago."

"And how many years were you married?"

She hesitated before answering, as if adding up the years. "I guess you'd say three years. For two of those years I idolized him." She sighed. "Then I grew up."

"Was he abusive?"

"Greg? No." She smiled, and changed the subject. "What we should be discussing is what happened this morning. After you left us at the car, what did you do?"

Jared retraced, as best as he could remember, his route from her car to the tree where she found him. He had a feeling she'd expected him to keep better track of his steps. He couldn't explain that his mind had been on ways to seduce her.

She laughed when he admitted that after he crossed the stream, he didn't have the slightest idea where he was. "So you were lost. What would you have done if we hadn't found you?"

"Just what I did. Hugged a tree."

His answer earned him a nod of approval.

By the time they were back at the pet shop, Jared knew exactly what the Captain had done to trail him. Laurie had it all down on the form on her clipboard, along with the weather conditions, the wind and temperature, the terrain they covered, and the time she started and ended the search. He understood that the exercise was important to her, but it also seemed she was using it to avoid talking about more personal matters.

Like them.

As she turned off the engine, she glanced at the clock on the dash. "Late as usual. Good thing Ruth's as enthusiastic about my search-and-rescue work as I am, or she would have called it quits long ago."

"You really have to go in now?"

"Yes." But she didn't open her door, and neither did he.

He angled his body toward hers, so that he could see her better. Even after a morning of traipsing all over the countryside, she looked lovely. Wisps of hair had pulled loose from her scarf and softly haloed her face. Her eyes were bright and her mouth so perfect, with or without lipstick. The more time he spent with her, the more beautiful she became. And the more intriguing.

"I—" They both started at the same time, then laughed.

"You go ahead," she said.

"I was going to say, I enjoyed myself today. This was interesting."

"Even getting knocked flat on your back?"

"Well, we don't need to repeat that, but any time you want me to get lost, just call."

"Sure."

The way she said it, he knew she wouldn't. Not that he was going to sit around and wait for her to call.

With the air conditioner off, the car was getting warm fast, the air heavy. Jared could hear the Captain panting in the backseat, see the rise and fall of Laurie's chest as she drew in shallow breaths. Cautiously he reached over and touched her shoulder. Her eyes widened, but she didn't move.

"What are you doing tonight after work?" he asked.

"I'm having dinner with Ruth and her husband," she answered quickly. "She said she had something important she wanted to discuss."

"What are you doing tomorrow then? It's supposed to be another hot day. I could pick you up around one or so, we could swim, lie around the pool . . . just *relax*."

Hope gathered in him when she didn't say no right away. He'd emphasized the word *relax*, but relaxing wasn't exactly what he had in mind. And considering the way her gaze traveled from his eyes to his mouth, he had a feeling she understood. He could swear her pupils got darker, and she would never know how she tempted him when she ran the tip of her tongue along her lower lip. He was ready to lean forward and kiss that lovely mouth when a cold, wet nose pushed against his arm.

His hand jerked on her shoulder, and she glanced to the back of the car. The mouth he'd wanted to kiss turned up in a smile. "What's the matter, Cappie? Tired of waiting for us to get out?"

The black dog whined and bumped Jared's arm again. There was no missing the message, and Jared pulled his hand away. He didn't know dogs could smile, but this one was.

Laurie opened her door. "I really do have to get in and help Ruth."

"What about tomorrow?"

Again she looked at him—wistfully, longingly—then she shook her head. "No, I shouldn't."

Disappointment snaked through him. "Shouldn't?"

"Can't," she corrected herself, and got out of the car to let the Captain out.

Jared also got out. "'Can't' and 'shouldn't' aren't good enough reasons, Laurie." Leaning against the car, he watched her move to the trunk. "Why shouldn't you? Why can't you?"

She didn't look at him as she pulled her gear bag from the trunk. "You know."

He didn't.

She slammed the trunk shut and started for her front door, her short legs eating up the distance with the speed of a roadrunner. He followed, his longer strides keeping him close. "Maybe I'm dense, but you're going to have to tell me."

Afraid she was going to get inside before she answered, he put a hand on her shoulder. "Laurie, stop. Look at me."

Reluctantly she did.

"Today went well, don't you think?" he said.

"Yes. Well, that is, if you don't count my dog knocking you out."

"I didn't boss you around or say anything to embarrass you, did I?"

"No."

"Didn't try to take over or tell you what to do, did I?"

"No."

If she'd been a dieter staring at a triple-layer

chocolate cake, the expressions flickering across her face couldn't have been more at odds. Slowly it dawned on him. She was attracted to him, yet appalled by that attraction. "Laurie, what is it?"

She barely whispered her answer. "Only a fool makes the same mistake over and over."

"You're no fool, honey." If anyone was, he deserved the title. He'd been making a fool of himself since the day he'd met her. And he knew he'd continue making a fool of himself. "What kind of a mistake do you keep making?"

"I . . ."

He thought she was going to tell him, then she shook her head. "I shouldn't have agreed to today. I've told you from the start I didn't want to get involved with you."

"You don't even know me."

"It doesn't matter." She avoided looking directly at him as she pulled a key from her pocket and opened her front door. "Thank you for helping me, but this has to be the last time we see each other."

The dog darted into the house, and Laurie tried to follow as quickly. Jared's hand, flat against the door, stopped her from closing it on him. Irritation laced his voice. "What is this all about? Why won't you go out with me? What are you trying to prove?"

"That I can stand on my own two feet."

"By running away? By denying what you feel?"

"I'm not running away," she argued. "I'm—I'm just not getting involved. Please, I can't explain. It's simply something about you. It's not your fault, but you remind me of someone."

"Your ex-husband?"

"Yes."

"Did he hurt you that much?"

"No. If anything, I hurt him." Once again she pushed against the door. "Look, I don't want to discuss it. Ruth is waiting for me, and I've got to get to work."

He could have forced his way in, but he let her shut him out. She was running scared, and to push her would only make matters worse. He would give her the night to think about today, about him. Then, in the morning . . .

At his car he dug into his pocket for his keys and had the door unlocked before he remembered Laurie still had something of his. *Maybe he wouldn't wait until morning after all,* he thought. Smiling, he turned around and headed back to her house.

She answered on the second ring of the doorbell. He was lounging against the doorframe, smiling rakishly, and the first thing he noticed was she'd been crying. Tears still glistened in her eyes. The moment she saw him, however, she tensed. "What do you want?"

"My wallet."

"What?"

"My wallet." He could tell she'd forgotten. "I gave you my wallet for the dog to smell. I need it now."

"Oh, of course." Turning her back on him, she walked to where she'd set her gear bag on the floor. She'd already taken the orange vest off and pulled her shirt tail from her pants. While she was busy looking for his wallet, Jared stepped into the house and quietly closed the door behind him.

"What is it about me that makes you afraid, Laurie?"

She straightened, his wallet in her hand. In her eyes he saw the longing. The confusion. "You're so much like Greg, it's scary."

"But I'm not him. I'm Jared North, a man you met less than two weeks ago. A man you really don't know." He closed the distance between them and put his hands on her shoulders. "Laurie, give me a chance. Give *us* a chance."

He had to lean over to kiss her, and she seemed small and helpless in his arms. A fragile flower to be protected and adored.

She brought one hand up to his chest. He thought she was going to push him away, but her fingers curled into his shirt. A little whimper escaped from her throat. "Oh, why can't I resist you?"

"Because I don't want you to."

There was no resistance when he lifted her into his arms and carried her to the couch. His mouth never left hers as he settled them down on the soft cushions. His kisses were eager, hungry. And like liquid fire, her body melted into his. He was aroused again, and so was she, her nipples taut, her breasts swollen.

He liked the way she fit against him, the way she arched her back and stroked her fingers through his hair. She'd given in to her desires and didn't pretend to be coy or reticent. She opened her mouth willingly to his tongue, then gave him hers.

He slid a hand under her shirt and rubbed her back. Hearing her throaty murmur of pleasure, he slipped his hand around to her front and touched her ribs. She pulled back a little, and he knew she was ticklish. It was something to remember, but tickling her was not what he wanted to do at the moment. His fingers moved on to the edge of her bra.

Beneath the satiny fabric, he could feel the warmth and fullness of her breast. Gently he cupped it, and she moaned. The material was in his way. He wanted to touch flesh, bare her to his sight. Holding her close, he fumbled behind her back to unclasp her bra.

A deep, guttural growl stilled his hands.

Standing next to the couch, his muzzle only inches from Jared's face, was the Captain, and the dog was not smiling.

"Laurie?" Jared whispered.

Like a kitten, she kissed his throat and kneaded the back of his shirt with her hands.

"Laurie?" he repeated, his gaze never leaving the dog.

Slowly, lethargically, she turned her head and looked to the side. Jared didn't move, and she laughed lightly. "Not now, Cappie. I don't want to play now."

The dog curled his lip, exposing his teeth, his eyes never leaving Jared's face.

"I don't think he wants to play, Laurie. He growled at me."

"He never growls at people."

"Sounded like a growl to me."

"Go on, now," she ordered her dog.

The Captain didn't move.

With a frustrated grumble, she disentangled herself from Jared and got up. "Come on, Cappie," she said. "He must think you're going to hurt me," she added to Jared as she hugged the dog. "Jared's not doing anything I don't want, boy."

The dog wagged his tail, but kept watching Jared.

Finally Laurie pointed at an overstuffed chair that had tape over most of its plastic seat. "Go lie down!"

With one last glance Jared's way, the dog obeyed and jumped onto the chair. Laurie shook her head. "Why is it all you males feel you have to protect me? Including my dog?"

Jared didn't try to answer. His own feelings seemed to be constantly torn between wanting to protect her and wanting to ravish her. At the moment ravishment was winning.

"Actually," she said, glancing at him, "it's probably a good thing Cappie did stop us."

Jared didn't agree. They'd been making progress, getting to know each other, at least on one level. He wanted to know more about her, on all levels. He patted the cushion next to him. "Come on back," he said, his voice still low with passion.

From the chair the Captain growled.

"Stop that!" Laurie ordered, her attention snapping back to her dog. She made certain he stayed where he was before she held a hand out to Jared. "I think you'd better go."

He stood slowly, his attention divided between Laurie and her dog. "Only if you promise to spend the day with me tomorrow . . . without your four-legged chaperon."

"I don't know."

"I think I deserve a chance to prove I'm different from your ex."

She touched his broad chest, her eyes troubled. "And what if you're not?"

Seven

Jared picked Laurie up at one. She greeted him with a tense smile. That she was ready and waiting relaxed him. He'd been prepared for the worst, either excuses why she'd changed her mind or no one at the house.

"Hi," he said softly, and dropped a quick kiss on her forehead. "You look nice."

Red was a good color for her, he decided. He liked the way it brought out the rosy hue of her cheeks and made her eyes look even darker than usual. He also liked the amount of flesh the simple sleeveless sundress showed and the way it accented her graceful, swanlike neck, her smooth, slender arms, and her shapely legs. Even with a neckline that came up to her collarbone, the dress was sexy as hell, hugging her breasts just the way he'd love to.

She followed the direction of his gaze and laughed nervously. "We look patriotic."

With him in navy shorts and a white top, he supposed she was right. "Ready?"

"Just let me get my tote bag."

The Captain was sitting by her bag, his gaze fixed on her, his tail brushing the carpet with an expectant wag. "No, you've got to stay," she said firmly. She glanced back at Jared. "Cappie always thinks he should be able to go anywhere I go."

She slipped on a pair of dark glasses—their enormous size dwarfing her face—picked up the tote, and motioned for Jared to leave first. She followed, slowly pulling the door closed, all the while talking to the dog. Just before the door clicked shut, the Captain gave three quick barks, then was silent.

"He's telling me to hurry back," she said.

"Or he's warning you to keep an eye on me."

"Should I?"

Should she? Jared asked himself. He wanted her more than he'd imagined he could want any woman, but he was no tomcat on the prowl, ready to pounce on her. "I'd never do anything you didn't want."

He wasn't sure, but as she walked past him toward his car, he'd swear she said, "That's the problem."

He held the door for her, and she patted the leather seat and nodded appreciatively before sliding in. "This is a first. I've never ridden in a Cadillac before. Wait until I tell Charlie."

"Charlie?" That was a new name to him.

"My stepfather." She twisted around to check out the interior. "He's always talking about someday owning a Caddie, but if I know Charlie, he'll be driving a Ford till the day he dies, cussing it and loving it."

When Jared got in, Laurie was still investigating the car. The moment he turned on the engine, she leaned over to read the computerized messages on the dash. "Driving this must be a lot like flying an airplane."

"In many ways they're similar."

She sat back and stared at him. "You know how to fly a plane?"

"Just the little ones. I learned a few years back."

Laughing, she relaxed against the seat. "Maybe you're right. Maybe you are different from Greg. He wouldn't go up in a plane if his life depended on it. Shoot, he doesn't even like to drive."

Jared was glad to hear it. The more she found different between him and her ex, the better. Or at least he hoped it would work for the better. Pulling out of her drive, he headed toward his house.

Norton was like many southern Illinois towns— small and rural, with a conglomeration of antebellum homes, sumptuous public edifices, modest houses that utilized native stone and hardwoods, and lots of trailers. On a summer Sunday afternoon, after all the church services had ended, the downtown area was dead, but the neighborhoods were alive with activity. Kids played baseball, softball, football, and soccer, and those who didn't play rode bikes, swam, or simply ran through sprinklers to keep cool.

The adults did less. A few energetic souls mowed their lawns, but most sat—in front of their televisions, on bleachers watching the ball games, on porches, or on lawn chairs. They sat and they talked: about what team was best, who was doing what, the weather, how the farmers were faring, and life in general. It was the way it had been in Norton for as long as Jared could remember and was how it would probably be for a long time to come.

His home was located in the newest section of town, where the houses were spaced far apart, and expansive lawns and high fences put a psychological as well as a physical distance between the residents and those driving by. For Joann, Jared had designed a home that combined function with understated elegance. There were no stairways to climb, rooms were clustered to save steps, and everything was convenient. Yet walls of windows gave the sense of lightness and space, and natural hardwoods, field stones, and polished marble blended in perfect harmony.

The moment Laurie stepped inside, Jared watched her, waiting for her reaction. Like Alice in Wonderland, she looked around the front foyer with an awed expression on her face. The only word she said was, "Wow."

"Do you like it?"

"Do I like it? This place is gorgeous. You've even got an indoor swimming pool."

"I had the Plexiglas dome put over it so that Joann could swim year round."

Laurie turned away from the window that looked out onto the swimming pool, pulled off her dark glasses, and wandered into the living room. Slowly she walked past the velvet sofa to the marble fireplace. She drew a fingertip over the mantle, grinned, and looked back at him. "Your home is a far cry from mine. Not a magazine out of place, no forgotten coffee mugs on the end tables, not even a speck of dust."

"My housekeeper, Maggie—Maggie Goodwin—is the one who gets the credit for the way this place looks. Monday through Friday she works here, making sure I have food in the refrigerator and meals I can pop into the microwave, picking up after me, and keeping things tidy in case I bring a client or business associate by. I also have a gardener, Artie. Between them, they more or less do everything."

"Must be nice. I would think I'd died and gone to heaven if I could afford to hire people to clean my house and cook my meals."

"How's your pet shop doing?" From things she'd said, he didn't think it was doing that well.

"Some days are better than others." She sighed,

and crossed over to the dining room. Obviously curious, she picked up the pewter candlesticks, smelled the flowers in the vase on the table, and ran a hand over the tops of the oak chairs. On the wall by the door to the kitchen was a full-sized painting of Joann. Laurie stopped and stared at it.

"This was your wife?" she asked.

"Yes." He moved closer. "It was painted two years before she died."

"She was pretty. Very sophisticated-looking." Laurie turned and faced him. "Did you love her?"

"Yes." He wouldn't deny it, no more than he would deny the growing feelings he had for Laurie.

"Was she as tall as she looks?"

"Joann was five feet six."

Laurie measured him with her eyes. "Just the right height for you."

"There's nothing wrong with your height."

"Not unless you live in a world where everything from kitchen cupboards to grocery shelves are designed for the woman of average height and you're way below average."

"Maybe so, but people of average height aren't as cute as you are."

Laurie frowned immediately, and he realized *cute* might not have been the right word to use. "Is that what you're looking for, Jared? Someone little? Someone you can dominate? Someone who'll make you feel young again?"

"No." He closed the distance between them and cradled her face in his hands. "When I met you, I wasn't even looking for anyone. Or at least I didn't think I was."

She put her hands over his and gazed intently at him. "The first time we met," she said seriously, "you told the sheriff I looked like a child. You ordered me not to help look for your niece."

How he wished he'd never said any of those things. It hadn't stopped Laurie from searching for

Susie, and now it was haunting him. "I was concerned for your safety. Is that wrong?"

"You said I looked young for my age."

"You do. Most women would take that as a compliment."

"Maybe." She didn't sound convinced.

"Look, I was wrong that night. You did an excellent job. I've told you that. What more can I say to convince you that I see you as a capable woman?"

"I don't know." She pulled away from him and walked back to the entryway. There she looked out at the pool. "Maybe I'm the one with the problem. Maybe I'm looking for trouble where it doesn't exist." Turning toward him, she smiled. "So, are we going to go swimming, or what?"

The "or what" sounded good to him. "Whatever you'd like."

"Where do I change?"

"You can either use my bedroom or the guest bedroom."

She didn't hesitate. "The guest bedroom will be fine."

He'd hoped she would choose his room.

At the doorway to the guest room he gave directions. "Bathroom's next door. You'll find towels there. Do you need any help?"

She was already pulling the red scarf from her hair. She glanced at him, and her hand stilled. "I do know how to dress myself."

"It was the undressing I was interested in."

She laughed nervously, her eyes never leaving his. "I think maybe we'd better get to know each other a little better first."

By the time Laurie came out of the house, Jared was swimming laps. He needed to, to work off the frustration building within him. He saw her as he made his turn, and his stroke died in the water. Leaning against the edge, his breathing strong and even, he stared at her.

She was wearing the oversized sunglasses and a one-piece bathing suit that was little more than blue Lycra molded over a perfect combination of womanly curves. The top and bottom were connected by a thin strip of fabric down the center of her body, leaving her waist exposed on either side. Staring at her, he remembered the feel of her breasts, their softness, and all the benefit he'd gained from swimming laps was lost. *His idea to go swimming was ridiculous*, he thought. Italian briefs, no matter how fashionable, were not designed for a man with an active libido. And lately his had been far too active.

Laurie entered the water with a low, clean dive, surfaced, and swam toward him. Her strokes were strong and sure until she came near the edge. There she stopped, leaving some distance between them. "Your pool is nice. I expected the standard aboveground model, not an in-ground as big as my house, all under glass and temperature controlled."

"Swimming was one of the few exercises Joann could do. I designed this so that she could get a good workout and swim, whether it was zero or one hundred degrees out."

Laurie sank straight down, her hair floating out over the surface as her head went below the water line. She bounced once, twice, her head bobbing above the water each time. Finally she came back up, shaking her hair from side to side like a dog, spraying him. "About five and a half feet deep, I'd guess."

"Five feet three inches at its deepest point," he corrected her. "I wanted it so that Joann could get her head above water if she ever felt tired and had to stop."

Laurie laughed. "Good thing you weren't designing a pool for me. You would have had a wading pool."

He grinned, and glided toward her. Her hair was clinging to her face now, droplets of water beading on her lashes and dripping down her cheeks. Her lips were moist and tempting. "Laurie . . ." he reached out and touched her shoulders. "If you want me to keep my hands off you, you'd better say so now. Otherwise I'm going to kiss you."

She was treading water, kicking her feet in a bicycle motion and rotating her arms to keep her head above water. Breathlessly she said, "What I think is I'm in over my head."

"Maybe we both are." Cupping her face in his hands, he held her up and gently brought her to him. He kissed her—as thoroughly and lovingly as he knew how, tasting the chlorine on her lips and the sweetness of her mouth.

She stopped kicking her feet and wrapped her arms around his neck. Her body rubbed against his, exciting him even more than he'd been before, and he was surprised the heat inflaming his body didn't raise the temperature of the pool to the boiling point.

"I want to make love with you," he said, slipping his fingers under the top of her bathing suit. Her breasts gave a little under the pressure.

"And if I say no?" Her question was a husky whisper as she tilted her head back, her eyes opened wide and fixed on his face.

"I'll keep my promise. I won't do anything you don't want. But it will be hard." He brought her hips against his, the outline of his erection not something either of them could ignore.

"Very hard," she agreed, and rotated her hips in a slow, seductive pattern.

"Oh, ho," he groaned, not quite certain who was

seducing whom. "Keep that up and I'm not sure I'll be able to keep my promise."

"Do you really want to make love with me, Jared?"

He was practically shaking, and almost laughed that she felt the need to ask. "You'd better believe it."

She ran her fingers through his wet hair. "I don't make you think of your little girl?"

"I don't have a little girl." He kissed her neck, then her shoulder. He wanted to kiss all of her.

"You don't feel you have to protect me?"

His chuckle was low and seductive. "Not at all."

Whatever answers she was looking for, he must have been on target, for she stopped questioning his motives and kissed him squarely on the mouth. No temptress could have aroused him more, and he hoped like hell she wasn't one who led a man on, then changed her mind. For all his promises, he wasn't sure he would be able to stop if they went much farther.

He eased the top of her suit down, all the way to her waist, freeing her breasts. For a moment he gazed at them, marveling at the way the water magnified their creamy beauty, then he drew her close, bringing her body against his.

Her nipples were erect, and the moment they touched his skin, jolts of electricity shot through him. He was driving himself crazy just holding her, yet he loved the feel of her. Her smell. Her taste. "Laurie," he said, shocked at how hoarse his voice had become, "I know you said you wanted us to get to know each other, but I want to be inside of you, to be a part of you."

She groaned. "I—I want that too."

He raised her higher in the water and licked droplets of water from her satiny smooth skin, then kissed each breast. Taking a hard, firm nipple into his mouth, he reveled at the deep, guttural moan that escaped from her lips. She was unabashed in her pleasure, undulating in his arms, and he knew neither of them cared how much they knew about the other. This was a basic need. A primitive yearning.

His lips reclaimed her mouth while his hand slid over her body, getting to know the lean lines of her ribs, the narrow width of her waist, and the curve of her hips. She was soft and womanly, and he pushed the clinging material of her bathing suit lower, exposing the triangle of fine hairs between her legs.

Supported by his arm, Laurie was also free to touch him. And she did, her hands rubbing over his shoulders and down his arms, then back up again. She made little mewling sounds, even as she kissed him, and swayed back and forth, her breasts rubbing against the pale golden hairs that covered his chest.

The water carried the rhythm of their motions and lapped against the sides of the pool. Neither of them was aware of anything but the pure pleasure of being touched and touching—until a small voice shattered their solitude.

"Hi, Uncle Jer. Mommy said I could go swimming."

Laurie gasped and wiggled, dropping most of her body beneath the protective cover of the water. Jared groaned and looked toward the house. Standing at the edge of the pool, already in a bathing suit, was Susie, her silvery-blond hair hanging down past her shoulders.

"Where's your mother?" Jared snapped.

Laurie answered for the little girl. "I see her. She's coming through the front door right now."

"Damn!" He tried to help Laurie pull her bathing suit up, but what had gone down so easily now refused to cooperate. The material bunched at her hips, slipped away from his fingers, and he could see Becky was heading toward the door that led out to the patio. Not only that, Susie was coming down the steps into the water.

"Let me go," Laurie whispered.

He didn't want to. He wanted to hold on to her forever, keep her close. He wanted time to reverse, for Becky to go away, and for Susie to get out of the water.

"Jared, please, let me go," Laurie repeated, desperation straining her low voice.

He let her go, but not willingly. His eyes darting between Susie and the woman who sank beneath the surface of the water, he suppressed an urge to bellow like a thwarted bull.

Susie began swimming toward them, her strokes a combination of the dog paddle and the breaststroke, her little head held high above the water. Becky walked through the patio door, a baby carrier in her arms, a diaper bag and over-sized straw bag slung over one shoulder. "Tom's going to be out in the fields all day," she called to him, "so we decided to come over and visit you. I—"

She stopped, and Jared knew why. He heard Laurie surface close behind him, felt the spray of water when she shook her head and the touch of her small hand on his shoulder. She coughed and wiggled, her front bumping against his shoulder blades. He actually felt when the top of her suit snapped back into place.

"You remember Laurie?" he asked his sister. "Laurie Crawford? The woman with the dog who found Susie when she wandered off?"

Laurie pushed herself away from his back and swam around to his side. Becky's gaze jumped from her to Jared's face and back to Laurie.

"I—I didn't know . . ." she stammered awkwardly, shifting the baby and carrier to a more comfortable position on her hip. "I didn't realize you had company. Susie, come back out. Uncle Jared is busy. We can't stay."

Susie was halfway across the pool, her arms splashing water around her head. Whether she didn't hear or simply chose to ignore her mother, Jared wasn't sure, but it was clear Susie wasn't going to turn around and get out.

"You don't need to go," Laurie said. "We were just swimming. I don't have a pool, and Jared offered his. It's been so hot, I couldn't turn down the invitation, but the more the merrier." She turned toward Susie. "She swims very well."

"A little mermaid," Becky said, though she was looking at Jared, waiting for him to say something.

What he wanted to tell her was to get his mermaid niece out of the pool, turn around, and go home to her farm and her husband. Instead he forced a smile. "If I know our little mermaid, she won't get out of this water until she turns into a prune. You might as well put my nephew down and join us."

"If you're sure . . ." Becky still waited, not moving.

"I'm sure." He looked at Laurie and found her watching him. "Later," he mouthed. Later they would finish what they'd started, would fully explore the pleasures they'd only begun to tap.

Susie swam past Laurie and directly to Jared. Her cherub face beaming, she wrapped her small arms around his neck and gave him a wet kiss. "I made it, Uncle Jer."

Her legs dangled down past his waist, and her toes brushed the hard bulge beneath his swim suit. Quickly he shifted her to his hip. "I'm glad one of us did," he grumbled, and heard Laurie laugh. Then, more like the type of mermaid he'd like to come across, Laurie dove under the water and swam to the opposite side of the pool.

• • •

Becky joined them in the water for a few minutes. "Just long enough to get wet," she said before getting out to check on her son. Laurie followed her, going over to look at the sleeping baby. By the time Jared was relaxed enough to step out, the two women were stretched out on chaise longues, talking like old friends. With a warning to Susie to stay in the shallow end, Jared went inside the house. He returned fifteen minutes later wearing a loose-fitting pair of shorts and carrying a tray of chips, cut vegetables, and the dip Maggie always kept in the refrigerator. He also had an assortment of sodas and a six-pack of beer.

"See . . . he brings food," Becky said when he neared the table by her side. "I told you he looks after me like a mother hen."

"Who's a mother hen?" he asked, setting the tray on the table. "What would you like, a beer or a soda?" he asked Laurie.

"A diet soda." Her glance briefly dropped to the front of his shorts, then back up to his face. She smiled and took the can he handed her.

"*You* are a mother hen," Becky said, also reaching for a diet soda. "I was telling Laurie how you were always watching over me when I was growing up, always getting me out of scrapes, making sure I got to the places I was supposed to go."

She glanced at Laurie. "Our mother is one of those women who joins every charitable cause in the universe. Show her a picture of a starving child and she'll spend hours raising money to feed it, but when it came to her own children, she wasn't around too much. And Dad was always busy with the business. Much as I griped at the time, I do appreciate the way Jared kept an eye on me." She patted his leg. "You may be a little overprotective, but I love you."

"I am not overprotective." He certainly didn't need Laurie thinking that, not the way she seemed to hate the idea of anyone being the least bit protective of her. "I'm just . . ." He couldn't think of a word to describe what he considered himself to be.

"You're just overprotective." Becky winked at Laurie. "But maybe he's had a right to be. What's a guy to do when he's saddled with a sister who's twelve years younger than he is and a wife who won't admit she has a weak heart?" She quickly looked at him, then back at Laurie. "He has told you about Joann, hasn't he?"

"He has." Laurie smiled up at him. "See, I'm not the only one who thinks you're overprotective."

"I am not overprotective," he grumbled, and grabbed a beer from the six-pack. With a snap he opened it and took a long draft of the cold liquid, letting the bubbles tingle his tongue before swallowing.

Becky grinned. "He's that way with you too?"

He scowled at his sister, and the look in her blue eyes said he'd be doing a lot of explaining later about what he'd been protecting Laurie from.

"He tries to be," Laurie said.

She kept watching him, he noticed. In her dark glasses he saw only his image, not her eyes or what they were expressing. Pulling a chair up next to her, he sat down. Maybe he'd have to behave himself with his sister and niece around, but that didn't mean he couldn't enjoy looking at Laurie, couldn't take pleasure in an occasional touch.

"So, how is the pet-store business going?" he asked, sliding a cold fingertip down her arm.

She shivered and took in a quick breath. "You want the good news or the bad?"

"Both."

"The good news is I may soon be sole owner of LaRu's Pet Shop. The bad news is I may soon be sole owner of LaRu's Pet Shop." She hesitated a moment, then continued. "Last night during dinner my partner hit me with the announcement that her husband has been transferred to North Carolina and they're moving in two weeks."

"You don't sound happy," Jared noted. In fact she sounded and looked as if the weight of the world had just settled on her shoulders.

"It's hard to be happy when all I see are negatives," she said. "A woman who's been my best friend for almost five years is going to be living a thousand miles away. Our shop . . ." She sighed. "Well, let's just say Ruth has the business savvy. My strength has always been working with the customers and knowing what to order, where to get it, and whom to ask if I didn't know. When it comes to keeping books and paying bills, I'm a failure . . . much as I hate to use that word. Greg said I'd never make a go of this. Looks like he may be right."

Before Becky had a chance to ask, Laurie explained. "I'm divorced. My ex still thinks I'm a child who couldn't possibly succeed at anything without his help."

"Some men are that way," Becky said, looking directly at Jared.

He raised his hands, the beer in one of them. "Hey, I just make suggestions. Not that you ever listen to any."

Becky leaned closer to Laurie. "He tries reason if you don't do what he suggests. If that doesn't work, he raises his voice. Then if that doesn't work, he'll walk off, as if you've hurt him deeply and he doesn't care what you do."

Jared could see Laurie's eyebrows rise behind her glasses, and he remembered how he'd acted in the cave after they'd found Susie and Laurie wouldn't sit on his lap. So, maybe he did turn away and walk off when negotiations reached a stalemate. He'd signed a lot of nice business deals by acting like he didn't care if he got the contract or not. Becky just didn't understand. With a grunt he hunkered deeper in his chair and stared straight ahead.

Susie was in line of his vision, but he didn't see her until she called to him. "You want to come in and play with me, Uncle Jer?"

"Not right now." Right now he wanted his sister to go home and for time to revert to the moment before Susie's interruption. He wanted to be alone with Laurie, kissing her, making love with her.

He might as well be asking for the moon, he thought. Becky didn't look like she had the slightest intention of leaving. In fact she seemed quite worried about Laurie's situation.

"Can't you just hire a bookkeeper for your shop?" she asked.

"What I'll have to hire," Laurie answered, "is a bookkeeper, a salesclerk, and a secretary—all in one, if I can find such a person. Which is doubtful, since this person is also going to have to be willing to work for peanuts. Ruth and I have been taking just what we need to survive out of the business and pouring everything else back in."

Which was good business sense, Jared mused. He tried to remember what Laurie's pet shop looked like. The day he'd stopped by, he'd been more interested in the owner than in the pet supplies. But he did remember one thing. "Why don't you have any pets in your pet shop?"

She turned her head his direction. "I don't believe in taking young animals away from their mothers just so that it's convenient for people to pick out a pet. And I won't handle birds, not when so many are taken illegally and die in transit. We do have fish, at least the common ones, and guinea pigs and mice, along with lists of reputable dealers and breeders. Mostly we sell pet food, supplies, and books."

"And there's enough business in that to make a living?" Never having owned a pet, he didn't know.

"I thought there was." She sighed. "Ruth and I decided to open a pet shop here in Norton because there were none in this area—not unless you drove to Carbondale or some of the towns in that direction. What I'm beginning to suspect is there was a reason there were no stores—no business."

It was her turn to stare out across the pool, beyond the Plexiglas wall and neatly manicured lawn he used as a putting green, to the stately pines that created the distant border of his property. What she was seeing he didn't know.

"You ought to let my brother help you," Becky said. "When it comes to operating a business, this man is the best." She leaned across Laurie and gave his leg a poke. "See, big brother, I'm not always putting you down."

Laurie said nothing, but Jared felt her resistance to the idea just as surely as if she'd pushed him away. Perhaps Becky also felt it, for she went on, extolling his virtues.

"You are not sitting next to a man who simply stepped into a cushy job. Not with our dad. Jer had to work to get where he is now. You've held every job there is at North Machinery, haven't you? From janitor to head honcho."

"Just about," he said absently, still watching Laurie. He knew it wasn't his experience that she was worried about but the idea of his taking over. Casually he caught some of her hair between his fingers, the damp strands catching the sunlight and turning to burnished gold. "You're safe. Running a pet shop is not on my list of things to do."

"Maybe not," Becky persisted, "but that business degree from Harvard must have taught you something about how to help a small business survive."

"You know what Dad always said about any business that depended on something that—" He stopped himself, glancing at Susie. She was playing with a windup turtle, but he had a feeling she was listening to every word they were saying. He chose his carefully. "My father didn't feel investing in anything that made excreta was a good idea."

Becky laughed. "Nicely put, big brother, even if I'll have to explain that word later to someone with big ears. And Dad still feels that way. He's always telling Tom to get rid of the farm, that it's too risky. Which is probably right, farming is risky. What he doesn't understand is, it's what Tom loves to do."

"Well, if I could do what I love doing," Laurie said, "I'd be training search-and-rescue teams. But that doesn't make money. It costs money. And running a pet shop is the next best thing I know how to do." Decisively she pulled her sunglasses off and sat up. "I think I'll hit the water again."

Swinging her legs off the chaise longue, she stood and walked toward the pool. She crouched beside Susie and laughed when the child made her toy turtle do a trick. Hypnotically Jared stared at her.

"She's nice," his sister said quietly.

He nodded.

"I'm sorry we interrupted your afternoon."

So was he.

"Have you told her?"

Eight

Jared faced Becky. "Told her what?"

"That you're in love with her."

His sister had thankfully whispered the words. He couldn't believe she'd even said them. "Love her? I hardly know the woman. We met that night Susie wandered off."

Becky simply smiled.

He shook his head. "Little sister, you've been out in the sun too long."

"And you, big brother, have stars in your eyes. Believe me, I'm glad to see them there. We all loved and miss Joann, but it's time you found someone new."

"Who's this 'we'?" They were whispering like school kids, and he certainly didn't want Laurie overhearing what they were saying, but he did want to know who was discussing his love life.

"Mom. Tom. Grace."

He should have known his secretary would be one. And his mother. For the last two years both had been trying to marry him off. But to Laurie?

He didn't know her well enough, hadn't known

her long enough. Heck, with Joann it had taken him five years to fall in love. They were friends long before he even thought of making love with her. Friends and classmates.

With Laurie his attraction was almost over-whelmingly physical. It was lust, that was all. He wanted her body and she wanted his. And as soon as Becky left, they could get on with a little mutually satisfying lusting.

Not bothering to change from his shorts back into a bathing suit, Jared joined Laurie and Susie in the pool. For a while the three of them swam and played games of tag. He kept a watchful eye on his niece, but it was Laurie who held his attention. He had a feeling they could have been on a crowded beach and it still would have been the same. No one else could hold his attention as she did.

Laurie had said she liked muscular men, and he didn't hesitate to show off. Lifting Susie above his head, he turned slowly, letting her get a good glimpse of the bulging muscles in his arms and shoulders. His skin, he knew, glistened a tawny-tan under the afternoon sun. Susie giggled and squealed, but it was Laurie's smile that gave him pleasure; it was the undisguised desire he saw in her eyes, now minus sunglasses, that heated his blood.

There was no doubt about it, he felt lusty. The last time he'd been this horny, he'd been a teen-ager. Maybe his sister thought she saw stars in his eyes. More than likely it was hormones exploding.

By the time Laurie got out of the pool, Becky had the baby out of his carrier and was feeding him. Jared decided to stay in the water with Susie. If he didn't, the moment he stepped out, three females were going to be shocked. His shorts might have been loose earlier, but wet and clinging to his body as they were now, they would clearly show the direction his thoughts had been taking.

It wasn't until his sister had finished feeding Todd and Laurie had taken the baby, that he felt it safe to leave the water. "Anyone want another soda?" he asked, quickly grabbing a towel and wrapping it around his waist.

Becky glanced at the watch she'd laid on the table. "Sounds good to me, then I think the kids and I had better head back to the farm."

That was the best news he'd heard since her arrival. More than ready to see his sister on her way, Jared headed for the kitchen.

Anticipation was a palpable sensation. He could taste it when he licked his lips. Never were three sodas and a beer transported from refrigerator to poolside with such speed. And if Becky hadn't already called Susie out of the pool, he certainly would have.

Mentally he willed his sister to drink faster and his niece to stop eating chips. Every minute seemed an hour. He concentrated on watching Laurie, memorizing every little quirk of her mouth, every funny face she made as she coaxed smiles from the baby on her lap. When his little nephew reached up, his tiny hand touching Laurie's breast, Jared envied the child.

"Well," Becky said, standing at last to take Todd from Laurie's arms, "now that we've drunk all of your soda, eaten all of your food, and cooled off in your pool, I think it's time we hit the road."

Laurie also stood. "I'm going, too, Jared. Becky and I talked about it while you were getting the sodas. It's silly for you to drive me home when she's going that way."

"I thought you'd stay for dinner," he said. *And more.* "Maggie left ham and a sweet-potato casserole." *We have some unfinished loving to tend to as well.*

"I really should get back and get to work. I mean, with having to take over the business and all . . ." Her words trailed off. "Thank you for this afternoon. I enjoyed myself."

"Did you?" He couldn't say he had. All his waiting, anticipation . . . for nothing.

"Yes. . . ."

He saw longing and need mix with hesitancy and uncertainty in those expressive eyes of hers. She wanted to stay, to go on from the point where they'd stopped, yet she was afraid to let herself.

"You what?" he asked.

"I—I think I'd better go home."

If his sister hadn't been standing next to them, watching and listening, he would have challenged Laurie to deny what she was truly feeling. He would have kissed her and chipped away at her fears. Instead he forced a stoic smile. "Whatever you say. Will you call me tonight?"

She shrugged, and he knew she wouldn't.

"Do you have my number?" he persisted.

"I know it," Susie said, and recited his telephone number from memory. "I get to call him for Mommy sometimes."

Becky grimaced. "And last month, according to our phone bill, she called someone in Texas. Now she can only make phone calls when Mommy is in the same room. Come on, Pumpkin." She gave Susie a gentle nudge away from the chips on the table. "Time to get your things together."

"And I'll get mine." Laurie turned to go back into the house, and Jared followed her.

He waited until she'd stepped into the spare bedroom and they were out of Becky's hearing range before he spoke. "You don't have to run off, you know. I told you I wouldn't do anything you didn't want, and I meant it."

"I believe you." She stuffed her clothes into her tote, slipped her sandals back on, then looked around the room. Certain she hadn't left anything, she walked toward him. She was about to leave.

"Stay," he pleaded softly.

Stopping in front of him, she touched his chest, her palm cool against his hot skin. "You scare me, Jared."

"Why? What have I done to scare you?"

"Nothing. It's—it's just that you're so sure of yourself, so capable."

"You'd rather I be a clumsy oaf?"

"No." She managed a smile, and whether she realized it or not, she was still touching him, twirling some of the blond hairs that covered his chest around her index finger. "It's just that being the kind of person you are, I know how easy it would be to let you take care of me, let you take over, make my decisions. But I can't let that happen, Jared. I've worked too hard at being independent. I can't—"

She didn't finish. Like a frightened fawn, she started to take off, but he caught her by the arm, stopping her. "Don't run away, Laurie." *He was losing her*, he thought, beginning to panic. "Maybe we both got a little carried away earlier this afternoon. Maybe we're not ready to make love yet. I can wait. Stay. Give us a chance to get to know each other. Give yourself a chance to find out I'm not all these things you seem to think I am."

"You ready?" Becky called from the entryway.

"Almost," Laurie yelled back.

"Please," he begged.

She shook her head, tossing her thick mane of sun-dried hair from side to side. "I can't, Jared. You don't know how much I—" She looked down at the white wool carpeting beneath their feet. "I just can't."

"Laurie, you're not being fair. To me . . . to us."

"Mommy's ready to go." Susie's little voice came from his side, and he looked down at his niece.

Wide-eyed with curiosity, she was watching both of them.

Laurie sighed, then laughed. "Maybe I will call you. We can talk then."

He supposed, if she was determined to leave, it was the only way they were going to get a chance to discuss the matter. "You promise?"

"I promise."

Five minutes later Laurie, Becky, Susie, and Todd were gone. His house was silent, and he carried the empty cans and bowls of chips and vegetables back to the kitchen. Loneliness carved a pit in his stomach that no food would ever fill. He stood in front of the picture of Joann, remembering how he'd felt when she was alive and how desolate he'd been after her death.

He'd thought he'd be content to live with his memories, that he'd never find another woman who would take her place. But the mind was unfair. His memories of Joann were fading, were getting tangled with new memories of a woman whose head barely reached his shoulders, whose brown eyes could snap with anger or burn with passion. Closing his lids, he whispered one small prayer. "Call me."

It was after nine before she did, when the light was rapidly leaving the sky. Hazy pink-tinged clouds took on irregular shapes, and the outlines of the trees edging his property were no more than a blur. From speakers mounted around the pool, the melancholy strains of Beethoven's *Moonlight* Sonata filled the enclosed area. Jared sat on a wrought-iron deck chair, still wearing the same shorts he'd swum in and a comfortable old sweat-shirt that was frayed at the cuffs. One leg crossed over the other, his elbows on the arms of the chair and his hands entwined, two fingers touching his lips, he looked out over the pool. He wasn't thinking of anything, and he was remembering everything. . . . Laurie's unabashed awe when she first saw the house, her enthusiasm when playing with Susie. How tender and loving she'd been with Todd. Her laughter. Her kisses.

The ringing of the telephone made him jump. His heart landed in his throat and his pulse pounded in his ears. He could feel the surge of adrenaline, the tension in his muscles, and he forced himself to wait until the second ring before he picked up the receiver. Nevertheless his hello was eager.

Hers was hesitant and as soft as a summer breeze. "Thanks again for a nice afternoon," she said. "I had a good time."

"You could have had a better time if you hadn't left so soon."

She laughed, self-consciously, he thought. "I needed time to think."

"And did you?" He certainly had.

"Yes." For a moment there was silence. He almost said something, but then she went on. "Your sister's really nice."

"If she'd been nice, she would have picked another Sunday to come for a visit."

Laurie laughed again, this time more spontaneously. "Good thing she didn't come ten minutes later."

"My niece would have gotten quite an education. I'm going to have to remember to lock my front door even when I'm home."

"The neighborhood where I grew up in Chicago, you wouldn't think of not locking your door anytime. That's one of the things I like about Norton. People are more trusting here."

"But you don't trust me."

"It's not you I don't trust." This time her brief laugh seemed directed at herself. "I wish I could tell you how confused I've been since meeting you."

"Try me."

"Maybe someday. Becky thinks the world of you, you know."

"And I feel the same way about her."

"All the way to my place she kept insisting I should take advantage of your business sense. She said if anyone could turn my pet shop into a money-making concern, it was you."

He said nothing. His sister had evidently gone to bat for him. That was like Becky.

"Jared?"

"Yes."

He could hear her draw in a deep breath and could imagine her pursing those sweet, lovable lips as she tried to think of the right words. They came slowly. "Would you help me?"

That had never been the problem, he thought. "The question is, will you let me help you?"

"You scare me, Jared."

"You keep saying that. What I don't know is why." He wished she were close, not on the phone. He wanted to hold her, reassure her. At her next words, though, he amended that thought. Perhaps having miles between them was good. For once she answered him honestly.

"It's hard to explain, but basically I'm afraid you're going to try to take over my life . . . and that I'll let you."

"Is that how it was with your husband? Did he boss you around? And did you let him?"

"According to Greg, he simply gave me advice. And yes, I was a good little girl and did what I was told. I don't want that kind of a relationship, Jared. Not ever again."

"I don't want to tell you what to do, but if you're asking for my advice . . ."

"I know." She laughed once more, and it was a

mixture of wry humor and ironic resignation. "It's a no-win situation."

"Not necessarily." *He was already gaining ground*, he thought. She'd called him, was opening up to him. And if he helped her with her shop, she'd have to spend time with him. "Why don't we give it a try?"

"Could we start trying tomorrow night, after work? Ruth's husband's transfer takes place in two weeks, and Ruth wants to know by then if I'll buy her out or if we put the place up for sale."

"Do you like Chinese food?"

"Does a Shar-Pei have wrinkles? Yes, I like Chinese. Why?"

"I'll pick some up after work and come by your place. While we eat, we can talk about the shop, then I can look at your books, and get an idea where you're at and what needs to be done."

Monday he should have worked after hours. They'd been having problems at the plant, but there was no way he was going to be late for this first meeting with Laurie. Besides, he had a good foreman. Bob Willis had reported the breakdown in the assembly line the moment it happened, and if anyone could get things going again, it was Bob. The man didn't need the boss hanging over his shoulder—especially when the boss wanted to be somewhere else.

Jared left at the same time Grace did. Both of them gasped at the heat the moment they stepped out of the air-conditioned building.

"I swear, it gets hotter every summer." Grace fanned herself with her hand, the perspiration rapidly beading up on her dark skin. "I imagine you're going home to your air-conditioned pool."

"Not tonight. I'm helping a friend decide if she should buy out her partner or sell her business."

Grace smiled knowingly. "This friend wouldn't be the one with the dog, would she?"

"Yes." He wondered how she knew.

"I understand she's very good with children. And a pretty good swimmer."

He groaned. "You've been talking to my sister, haven't you?"

Grace grinned. "Becky called this afternoon while you were with Bob looking at Line Two. She said she didn't want to bother you, she just wanted to apologize for barging in on you yesterday, and to tell you that next time she'll call first. She also wondered if her pep talk had worked. I wasn't sure what she meant, and you've been so busy all afternoon, I forgot to ask." Her dark eyes twinkled. "So, did it?"

Jared chuckled. With a secretary and a sister keeping tabs on him, a man didn't have a chance for a discreet love affair. "Next time you talk to Becky, tell her it worked. She convinced Laurie that I'm a wizard when it comes to saving businesses. Now I just hope I can live up to my reputation."

"I don't know about wizard, but you sure are a hard worker." Grace stopped beside her Buick Regal. "Just remember, all work and no play makes John a dull boy." She winked at him. "But then again, I don't imagine you'll be working *all* night."

It was past six when Jared knocked on Laurie's front door. The dog barked, and Jared remembered the last time the Captain and he were together. What chance did a guy have? If it wasn't his sister acting as a chaperon, it was a dog.

After two minutes Jared decided Laurie was still in the pet shop. He walked around to the side entrance, carrying a couple of bags of take-out food. The sign in the window said CLOSED, but the door was open.

Laurie was back by the register going over receipts. She looked up when the bell announced his arrival and simply stared at him as he walked toward her. Her hair was loose, golden-brown waves cascading over her shoulders. She pushed one side back, behind an ear, and absently ran the tip of her tongue over lips that held a mere trace of red lipstick. There was only one way to describe the look in her eyes. It was a look of hunger . . . and not for food. And it was the same look he was giving her.

As he neared the counter, she licked her lips again, then smiled. "You must be the delivery boy."

"Do I look like a boy?"

He felt as well as saw her gaze travel down over his body, and he knew exactly where it paused, if only for a second. She looked back up quickly, her blush giving away her thoughts. "I'll be just a minute," she said. "You can go into the house if you'd like."

"Thanks, but no thanks. Your dog has already told me what he'll do to me if I invade his territory."

"He what?" She frowned, then understood. "Oh, you went to the front door first. Don't let Cappie buffalo you. He's really a big pussycat."

"*Big* is the key word." *And if the Captain was a pussycat,* Jared thought, *he was sure the dog saw him as a rat.* "If you don't mind, I'll just wait until you're finished. Besides, it will give me a chance to look around."

He set the bags of food down on the counter. The aromas of fried rice and pork, ginger and soy sauce were already filling the small shop. Wandering around, he pretended to check out her inventory. It was all a sham. Laurie was the one he was studying.

She wore beige shorts that looked like a skirt,

two-inch brown heels that gave her legs a sleek appearance and her some added height, and a peasant-style blouse that was patterned with brown and yellow and black kittens. Her skin had a pinkish hue he hadn't noticed before, and though the color in her cheeks might be due to his presence, he didn't think she blushed on her shoulders.

"Get a little sunburned yesterday?" he asked, heading back toward the register.

"A little." She glanced his way, then down at the receipts. "I didn't realize I'd get a sunburn through that glass. You ought to see my back."

"I'd love to."

Her cheeks grew pinker. "Let me rephrase that."

He chuckled. "How much longer will you be?"

"Just about got it." Her hair had fallen forward, and she again swept it back, exposing her neck. Impetuously he leaned over and kissed her shoulder.

She jerked back. "Jared, I . . . we . . . If we're going to work together, if you're going to help me figure out what I should do with the shop, I don't think you should kiss me."

"You know we're going to be lovers, don't you?"

Her gaze dropped. "Don't say that," she whispered.

"Why? You look at me exactly the same way I look at you. We know how we react whenever we touch, or kiss. Maybe you think you can pretend this is strictly business, but I can't. I want to help you, but I also want to make love with you. Tonight. Tomorrow night. Whenever you're ready."

She glanced up at him again. "I really do need time to get to know you," she said earnestly.

He bent down and kissed her forehead. "You know I like kissing you. And that I like Chinese food. What else is there to learn about me?" He patted one of the take-out bags. "I, however, just realized there's something I don't know about you. Do you have chopsticks?"

"You're in luck. I do."

And she did, though it took her a while to find them. Jared was amazed she could find anything in her house. Her method of storing items seemed to be based on a "put it wherever you are" system. Even her dining table was buried under paper-work, magazines, and newspapers.

They decided to eat in the living room, and her coffee table—once she'd cleared off the books and magazines that had accumulated there—made a perfect table. Jared opened the containers and dished a little food from each onto their plates.

He was impressed by the Captain. Although the food was right at nose level, the dog never once bothered it. Nor did he growl or even show his teeth when Jared moved around the table to sit beside Laurie.

"He's not supposed to growl at anyone," she said when he mentioned that. "That could knock him out of being a search-and-rescue dog. Who wants to be rescued, then chewed up by their rescuer?"

He laughed and put his hand on her knee.

She tensed. "Don't you think we should get down to business?" she asked.

"I am." Touching her chin, he urged her face toward his.

For an instant her gaze fixed on his mouth, and he knew she wanted him to kiss her. Then she resisted his touch and turned away. "Pet shop business," she said swiftly. "How can I buy out my partner and not go under?"

He wanted to know why her eyes turned a darker brown every time he looked at her. Why his entire body went haywire whenever she was close. She, on the other hand, wanted to play it safe. She wanted to get to know him. Looking at the Captain, who was lying on the carpet half asleep, Jared realized why the dog wasn't growling. The beast knew he had nothing to worry about. Jared North was getting nowhere with Laurie Crawford tonight.

Not that night, nor the next night, nor the next. By the end of the week Jared knew more than he'd ever wanted to know about the pet-shop business. He'd gone over the books from the time Ruth and Laurie had opened the shop, talked to both of them, and called friends and business associates who gave him their opinions.

For Laurie to stay in her house and in Norton, she had to keep the business running. Since he wanted her to stay in Norton, he came up with a plan. He wouldn't say it was a truly objective plan, and he certainly didn't intend to present it to her in a sterile, businesslike atmosphere. He called her Saturday night, ready to make his pitch.

Her phone rang once, twice, then her recorded message came on. As soon as the beep sounded, he spoke. "It's Jared. Pick up the phone, Laurie. I've got something worked out and I need to talk to you."

In a second she was on the line. "Can I pay off Ruth and still keep the place going?"

"Yes, if you agree to my plan, you can."

"So, how do I do it?"

"You start by driving over to my place tomorrow."

"Jared, I'm serious. Ruth asked me today if I've decided what to do."

"I'm serious too. I have all the paperwork here at the house. See you at three? I have a golf game earlier."

He hung up before she could give him a reason why she couldn't. *The bit about the golf game was ingenious,* he thought. How could she argue about place or time when he was squeezing her into his

busy schedule? Not that he had a golf game scheduled, but he would find one.

He did call her back, though. This time after the
beep he left one short message. "Sweet dreams,
Laurie."

Nine

He did play golf early Sunday. By the time he reached the eighteenth hole, the temperature was only in the low seventies, the sky was slate gray, and a fine mist of rain had started to fall. It was a perfect afternoon to curl up with a good book . . . or woman.

Back at his house Jared showered and changed into gray slacks, a light-blue short-sleeved silk shirt, and loafers. He took time with his hair, using the blow-dryer. Pale shades of honey and straw topped his ears and collar. It was the strands of white that bothered him. Today he wanted to look youthful. Debonair. Virile.

Laurie arrived at ten after three. His nerves were strung as tight as a Stradivarius. She came in smiling, but it was a tense smile.

"So, how was your golf game?" she asked. "Did you finish before this rain started?"

"Just." He didn't mention his score.

"I had a good morning. I actually cleaned my house." She glanced at his living room and adjoining dining room. "Where do you want to work?"

"The dining room. Before we get started, would you like something to drink? A beer? Glass of wine? Soda?"

"A diet soda would be fine."

Why she always chose diet, he didn't know. There wasn't an extra pound on her. Even the baggy beige slacks and long-sleeved red top she had on didn't disguise her petite figure.

He hesitated before going for the soda and watched her wander to the windows that looked out on the pool and backyard. The rain was coming down in a steady drizzle, the drops dancing on the Plexiglas roof above the pool and rivulets of water running down the side that faced the backyard.

"We could go for a swim," he said. The idea of being in the water again with Laurie aroused him. But then, every thought about her aroused him.

She tried to laugh; it came out as a groan. She turned to face him. "I didn't bring my suit."

"You don't need one."

In the silence that filled the room, a pin dropping would have sounded like an explosion. He didn't think she took a breath. He knew he didn't. All he could do was stare at her and hope the forces driving him totally crazy were affecting her just as strongly.

When she found her voice, it was low and husky. "And after we go swimming?"

"We make love."

Her eyes never left his face, and the breath she did release was shaky. "I think maybe I need a glass of wine."

"And then?"

"And then we need to get down to business . . . the business of saving my pet shop."

He didn't want to talk business. Not yet. In the last week they'd spent hours talking about sales potentials, risks, and payment plans. He'd learned more than he needed to know about her pet shop and too little about her. He'd been the perfect gentleman, kept his hands to himself and his desires in check. He was tired of denying the way he felt. "Laurie, I want you. And if you'd be honest with yourself, you want me."

"Wanting isn't enough. There has to be respect, mutual interests, commitment, and . . ."

She didn't finish, but he knew what she wanted to say. Love. There had to be love.

He moved toward her—slowly. "I care for you, Laurie. Very much."

Cautious and uncertain, she voiced her doubts. "I've been married once and had one affair." Caution and uncertainty were clear in her voice. "Neither worked out."

"That doesn't mean we're doomed to failure." He touched her arm and felt her shiver. "Since I met you, I've wanted you."

Her eyes were so dark, her breathing uneven. "Laurie, I don't know if what I feel is love, and I can't guarantee a 'happily ever after' ending, but when two people excite each other as we do, something has to be right."

Out of habit his fingers pressed the pulse at her throat. She grinned. "You don't need to check. It's racing."

Taking her hand in his, he brought her fingers up to touch his own throat. "Mine is racing too. Along with my heart."

She freed her hand and rested it against his chest, then shook her head. "I can't believe this is happening. I thought I could resist you, that being around you would get you out of my system. Before I left my house, I actually had convinced myself that I could come here today and not be tempted. I thought I'd grown up and was over this obsession for an older man."

That hurt. "You consider thirty-eight old?"

Her little snort of disgust hurt too. "It's getting younger every year," she muttered.

"Meaning?"

She shrugged and walked away. In his living room she stopped, turned, and looked back at him. "Jared, how do you see me?"

"As a beautiful woman." He wasn't sure what she wanted to hear. "Sexy. Exciting."

She tried to smile. It was there for a moment, then gone. Shaking her head again, she sank down on his plush green-velvet sofa, kicked off her shoes, and curled her toes into the thick pile of the white carpeting. "I'm not beautiful, and I certainly don't see myself as sexy or exciting."

"How do you see yourself?" *Maybe that was the problem,* he mused, *her image versus his.* Walking into the living room, he positioned himself behind the sofa. Behind her. He wanted to let her work this out without interference.

"Good question," she said. Leaning her head back, she closed her eyes. "When I'm working with the Captain, I see myself as capable and in control. When I'm at the shop, I see myself as a good salesperson, congenial, informed, and energetic."

He'd agree with her assessment, especially the energetic part. It was a quality he'd admired in her from the start. "And with me?"

"Unsure of myself. Defensive. Out of my league."

He touched her hair. It was soft, luxuriant. Shades of oak mixed with ginger. "You shouldn't feel that way."

"Sometimes I also feel childish, and I don't want to feel that way, Jared. Never again."

"You're no child."

"Aren't I? When you touch me, excite me, I want to run away before I start caring too much. When you walk into my house and start talking about my business, I want to turn it all over to you and let you make the decisions." Tilting her head back, she looked up at him. "Even now. I want you to hold me close and tell me everything will work out, that I'm not about to make another mistake. Isn't that childish?"

Leaning over, he kissed her. The position might be awkward, but the feeling was good. He straightened and grinned. "If feeling that way makes you childish, then I must be childish too."

She twisted to face him. Confusion clouded her eyes and creased her forehead with fine lines. "I thought I had everything under control, that I didn't need a man, that my search-and-rescue work and the pet shop would be enough. Then your niece had to go and get lost."

"And we met." He moved around the sofa to sit beside her. He'd left her alone long enough. "I do want to hold you. And I do think everything will work out." He drew her close. "Plus, if we're talking about expectations changing, you've changed mine. You're looking at a man who thought he'd be content with the memories of a wonderful woman and marriage. Now, in the last two and a half weeks, I've had an erection so many times, you'd think I was a teenager. I can't function at work, all I want is to be with you, and if we're going to be honest, that golf game this morning was a waste of time. All because the only thing I could think about was getting back here and making love to you."

Her laughter was breathless, and she reached up and touched his face, her caress as feathery as the brushing of butterfly wings. "And I cleaned house this morning because I needed something physical to do while I thought of ways to stop you from making love to me."

"And did you think of a way?"

"No. I think my problem is I really don't want to stop you." Her hand traveled down the side of his face to his throat, then his chest. She didn't pause to take his pulse or feel his heartbeat.

He sucked in a breath when her fingers made it to his belt buckle, and when she touched him, he knew she was no child. Conceptual need became a hard reality, hormones exploded, and he groaned her name.

"Make love to me, Jared," she whispered, and rubbed her palm over the length of him. "Now, before I think about what we're doing."

Holding her hand, he led her to his bedroom, pausing only to make certain the front door was locked. The drapes covering the floor-to-ceiling windows that faced the pool were quickly closed, and the quilted comforter whipped off his king-sized bed. Laurie stood watching, her mouth a tense line. Before she had a chance for second thoughts, he kissed her and brought her down with him onto cool cotton sheets.

"Anything you like or don't like?" he murmured.

"I don't know." Her answer was shaky, her touch tentative. "I'm not all that experienced, Jared."

"If you're talking about numbers, neither am I." He tasted her lips, then deepened the kiss, slipping his tongue into her mouth. Past experiences didn't matter, he knew. This was new. Different. Exciting.

"Touch me," she begged, curling toward him.

"Gladly."

Her breasts, soft yet firm, fit his palms perfectly. She helped him remove her red top, then she rolled to the side so that he could get to the snap on her bra. Naked to the waist, she attacked the buttons of his shirt. Her breasts rubbed against his chest as she pulled his sleeves down his arms. He loved it. She twisted so that she could draw the clingy silk from his back, but he stopped her, catching a rose-hued nipple in his mouth.

Her moan came from deep within. Somehow she

still got his shirt off. He sucked, and she kneaded his arms with her fingers, arching her back and driving her hips into his.

He wanted to do everything at once, feel her velvety-soft skin against his, squeeze her hips into his, kiss her, nibble. Suck. Her sighs mingled with his groans. He touched; she responded. The scent of her body became stronger, more exciting, and the taste of her skin slightly salty. Shoes dropped to the floor, followed by slacks. Her skimpy, lacy white bikini panties offered no more coverage than his navy-blue briefs, yet he left them on, testing his resistance . . . and hers.

Neither lasted long.

She participated as an equal, not hiding her pleasure or curiosity. Her fingertips trailing over the outline of his arousal nearly drove him crazy, yet the moment she stopped, he wanted more. And her tongue . . . It tested his fortitude to its limits. He'd never realized his ears were so sensitive, or that his nipples were directly connected to the nerve endings up and down his sides. She grinned at his moan and teasingly pulled at the hairs on his chest.

"You're asking for it," he warned, and knew she knew it.

His satisfaction was realizing he had the same effect on her. His tongue peaked her nipples into hard nubs and brought forth cries of pleasure and a writhing of her hips. His hand between her legs found warmth and moisture, and his finger, delving deep, confirmed what he already knew. She was ready for him.

He wanted more than her readiness, though. He wanted her to need him as much as he needed her, to be half out of her mind with desire. Slipping her panties from her hips, he kissed her. She sucked in a breath, her legs tensing, and grabbed his shoulders, clinging to him as he urged her closer to the edge of insanity.

"Jared . . ." His name was a plea for release.

He took only a moment to remove his own briefs and get one of the foil packets he'd placed in his nightstand. Another moment to open it. He felt her gaze on him as he prepared himself. Looking down at her small hips, he said, "If I start to hurt you, stop me."

Her smile calmed his fears. He didn't want to ask how she knew there'd be no problem, yet he was glad she wasn't a trembling virgin. He was too near the edge, too tense. He wanted it perfect for her, but he was afraid he would fail.

"It's been a long time for me," he apologized, his body poised over hers. "I'm not sure . . ."

She reached up and cradled his face in her hands, her touch gentle yet possessive. "North, you worry too much."

It was the prod he needed. Gathering her to him, he mixed kisses with touches, rubbed himself against her, teasing her, until he was the one who could wait no longer. With a sigh of pleasure, he sank deep into her moist warmth.

"Oh, yes," he whispered. She was all he'd anticipated and so much more.

"Yes, do it. Do it." Eyes closed, her head rocking back and forth, her hair fanning out on the sheet, she repeated the words.

"Come for me," he pleaded, slipping his fingers between them to find where she was most sensitive. "Come with me."

He felt her tighten around him, and it was nearly his undoing. "Yes," he urged, forcing himself to remain still, his fingers continuing their delicate task.

"Oh, Jared." Her eyes opened and she stared up at him with surprise, her hands tightly gripping his arms. Her body began to tremble, then she cried out and thrust her hips against his. He felt the rhythmic contractions, the tightening and release. Then, head thrown back, body arched, he gave what he'd received.

His skin moist with perspiration, he collapsed beside her, then drew her close and kissed her. It was a few minutes before he could talk. "That, my love, was wonderful."

The sound Laurie made was close to a purr, and she curled against him like a kitten. Her hands traveled over his damp chest, then down his arms. He felt as though she were claiming him.

"We should have done this a long time ago," he said scattering little kisses across her face.

"I didn't know you a long time ago."

That seemed impossible. "I feel like I've known you all of my life."

She laughed. "Funny you should say that. Ever since I met you, I've felt the same way. Only I haven't been looking at it in a positive way."

"Maybe you should." He sat up, revitalized. "Let's go for a swim."

"In the buff?"

"Becky and Tom took the kids to Saint Louis. We're safe." Plus, he doubted his sister would ever again drop by unannounced. "And after we take a swim, I'm going to make love with you, again and again."

Actually, they didn't get out of the bedroom before they made love again. Then they swam . . . and made love. Finally, after a shower, Jared heated the lasagna Maggie had made and left in the freezer. He served it to Laurie with wine and candlelight and the soft strains of Mendelssohn coming from the speakers placed throughout the house.

By the time dinner was over, she was totally relaxed, her eyes half-closed and dreamy from the wine, her mouth a natural red and a little swollen from hours of being kissed. He knew he should be satisfied and that both of them were going to be sore the next day, but simply watching her lick the last trace of cheese from her lips made him want to kiss her again, make love with her again. If he'd thought getting her into his bed would get her out of his system, he'd been wrong. The lady was addictive.

And not just sexually, he admitted. He was addicted to her smile, her laugh, even her stubbornness. Everything.

If he was going to keep her around, though, he needed to help her with her financial problems. It was time to make his suggestion. He excused himself to get his papers, then returned and began his sell job.

"I've looked at the figures you gave me in every way I could possibly think of. I even asked a friend who acts as a consultant to small businesses what he thought you should do."

He paused intentionally, knowing what she would ask. She did. "What did he say?"

"That you should sell the house and pet shop."

Disappointment shadowed her expressive eyes. "And then do what? Tuck my tail between my legs and trot back to Chicago—to Greg—who's been telling me all along that this was a harebrained idea that would fail."

"No." He didn't want her turning to another man. He wanted her looking to him for help. "I want you to take on a new partner."

"Just like that?" She snapped her fingers. "It's not that easy, Jared. Ruth and I were friends long before we decided to become partners. Even so, we've had some differences of opinion. I don't think I could work with just anyone."

"So, pick a partner you can work with. Pick me."

The way her mouth fell open, he knew she hadn't expected that. But this wasn't an impulsive suggestion. He'd thought the matter over thoroughly. "I'm not independently wealthy, but I can afford to take a risk."

"Take a risk?" Her voice rose, and so did she, shoving her chair back from the table. "Great! you're offering to be my partner, but you see the pet shop as a risk."

He also stood, then decided that wasn't a good move. She might see it as him trying to intimidate her with his size. He sat down again. "Laurie, look at this reasonably. Your business is a risk. The country's in a recession. Pets are a luxury."

"Haven't you heard, people eat dog food during recessions. I'm probably going to make a fortune."

He doubted it. In Chicago there might be enough interest to make a go of a shop like hers, but he didn't want her in Chicago, he wanted her in Norton. "All I meant is I have some money that's not tied up, and I can afford to invest in your pet shop. I hope you sell lots of dog food and double my investment. In fact I've worked up some ideas that might help bring in more customers."

"You have some ideas." She enunciated each word carefully, her gaze never leaving his face. Then she shook her head.

Gone was the lover he'd known only an hour before. Before him stood a woman ready for war.

Laurie retreated, however, turning and walking straight toward the windows that looked out over the pool and his backyard. She was mumbling to herself, and he heard only the last two words. They sounded like, "Like him."

"Like who?" he asked.

She didn't look back. "Greg."

Jared bristled instantly. "I am tired of being compared to your ex-husband."

That brought her around. "Then stop acting like him."

Once again he came to his feet. "Here I thought I was helping you, that you'd be relieved to have the money you need to buy out your partner's interest. If you don't think your place is a risky investment, you haven't been paying attention to the figures you've been quoting me all week. You're barely making ends meet, and once Ruth is out of the picture, either you're going to have to give up your search-and-rescue work and devote one hundred percent of your time to the shop or you're going to lose the place."

"Oh, now I haven't been paying attention!" A ramrod couldn't have been straighter than her back. "Anything else you'd like to correct me on?"

"No." He didn't know what he was saying that was so wrong. He was giving her facts, that was all. She was the one getting all emotional.

For a moment she simply stared at him, then she looked back out the window. The clock in the living room ticked off the minutes and the rain continued to fall, as it had all afternoon . . . a gray, dismal drizzle that reflected exactly how he felt. Laurie said nothing, and neither did he. He'd already said too much.

When she did speak, her voice was almost a whisper. "Does it give you pleasure to know I have no choice?"

"I'm only trying to help." He'd said it before, and he meant it.

Finally she faced him again, shoulders back, chin raised. "I want time to think about this."

"That's fine with me." Though he knew she didn't have much time. Ruth wanted an answer soon.

"And," she went on, "if I decide to let you buy out

Ruth's half of the business, this has to be done right. I want a contract between us. I want what aspects of the business you have control over and what I have control over spelled out."

"I have no problems with that. What are you so afraid of, Laurie?"

"That you'll take over."

He grinned, even though her fear wasn't funny. "I've got my hands full running North Machinery. I know close to nothing about animals. Why would I want to take over your place?"

"Why do you even want to invest in it?"

"Because I don't want you leaving Norton."

He'd been honest, but the way she looked at him, he had a feeling she was trying to ferret out another motive. Finally she nodded. "Maybe this is a test. A chance for me to prove that I really have changed."

"I don't understand."

"Neither do I, but I sure hope you're not expecting me to jump at your suggestions just because I jumped into your bed."

He suppressed a sigh of frustration. When would she trust him? "The only thing I expect is honesty . . . in our business dealings and in our personal relationship."

"I've been honest." She didn't look away. "I've told you from the very beginning that you scare the hell out of me."

Ten

She accepted his offer, as he'd hoped she would, and they drew up a formal contract. Since Ruth and Laurie had been equal partners, that was how Jared was listed. Laurie also insisted on spelling out the terms if either wanted out of the arrangement.

He wasn't ready to think about ending their relationship. It was just beginning, and every day he spent with her, he became more convinced that there would be no ending.

The month of August became a time when they learned about each other. She listened to his tapes of Bach, Beethoven, and Brahms, then tried to explain to him the difference between hard rock and the kind of rock and roll she liked. On weekends they'd swim, and he showed her how to swing a golf club. She soon had him jogging. He straightened her living room; she gave his house a lived-in look.

With their busy schedules, finding time to be together wasn't always easy, but Jared began regularly stopping by the pet shop after he left work.

Sometimes he even left the plant early to help Laurie stock shelves, check inventory, or brainstorm new ideas. His secretary quickly noticed the change in his routine. As he passed her desk on his way out one Friday afternoon, Grace glanced at her watch.

"Going to check on your investment?" she asked.

"As a matter of fact, yes. Laurie and I are working on a new ad campaign. I think if more people know her philosophy about not caging animals, we might interest some of the animal-rights people into stopping by."

"What about the search-and-rescue work? Is she still doing that?"

"She runs with her dog every day, just to keep both of them in shape, and works him on training exercises at least four hours a week. On Sundays we've taken him to downtown Springfield, to the fluorite mines over near Rosiclare and to Becky's farm, so that he'll be accustomed to all sorts of situations. There hasn't been a call for her since July, though."

"She's good for you," Grace said bluntly.

Jared couldn't disagree.

Life had taken on a new zest since he'd met Laurie. He felt invigorated, energized. Which was amazing, considering how many nights he hadn't gotten to sleep until midnight. Sex had to be a stimulant.

The shop was closed when he arrived, which was wrong. According to his watch, it was only four-thirty. Laurie was scheduled to work until six, then Donna, a senior at Norton High, would take over. LaRu's now stayed open until nine. That was one of his suggestions Laurie had agreed to.

He opened the pet-shop door with his key and walked straight through to the kitchen. "Laurie?" he called.

The sink faucet dripped and the refrigerator hummed, but the house was silent. No rock music—hard or soft—assailed his ears, no whistling, no dog barks. He knew then that she was on a rescue.

Returning to the shop, he found her note propped up on the cash register. *Bank robbed in Harrisburg. They want to see if Cappie can track the robber. See you later. P.S. Tell Donna I didn't have time to cash out.*

It looked like she'd signed it *Love, Laurie*, then erased the word *Love* and written *Yours* over it. Jared stuffed the note in his pocket. If she was in Harrisburg, that was where he was going.

He was about to leave the shop when he heard the phone in the house ring. On the hope that it was Laurie, he dashed back into the kitchen. Her answering machine was already running when he picked up the receiver. His breathless hello was answered by a gruff male voice. "Who the hell are you?"

"Jared North. Who are you?"

"Greg Crawford, Laurie's husband."

The words hit like a fist in the gut. "Her husband?"

"Well, ex-husband, I suppose, though she'll be back. My baby always comes back, sooner or later."

Jared could breathe again. "I wouldn't plan on it this time."

"What did you say your name was?"

"North." Maybe he shouldn't sound so cocky, but he couldn't help himself as he added, "Jared North, Laurie's fiancé."

"Fiancé?"

"Yes." Okay, maybe it was a little lie, but marriage did seem a natural next step to their relationship.

For a long moment there was silence on the other end of the line. Jared could hear the man breathing—deep, frustrated breaths—then a clearing of the throat. "Is Laurie there?"

"No, she's out on a rescue."

"She's still into that?"

"Yes, she's still into that." Jared tried to get an image of the man. He sounded big. Burly. Not highly educated, but not dumb.

"Well, tell her I called."

"I will." And he would. He wanted to know more about the man Laurie had been married to, a man who still called. A man who thought she would come back to him.

Even though Harrisburg was a town of only ten thousand, finding Laurie and the Captain turned out to be a lot more difficult than Jared had expected. There were banks everywhere—First Bank and Trust, First National, Harrisburg National. Main branches and drive-ins. He drove past four before he saw the white-and-gold state police car. An officer stood in front of the automatic teller machine, and Jared pulled his Cadillac into the parking area.

"Machine's broken," the officer said as Jared approached. The man's wide-legged stance and the gun strapped to his hip was enough to discourage most from challenging his statement.

"I don't want to use it," Jared said. "I'm looking for a woman and a dog. They're tracking a robber. I'm—I'm supposed to be helping her."

The officer nodded to his right. "They're over near the fairgrounds. The punk blew a tire and took off on foot. He's either hiding in one of the buildings or in the woods."

"What's the fastest way to the fairgrounds?" Jared was already backing toward his car.

"Take North Main to Dorris Heights. You can't

miss it." The officer looked him up and down. "You really with that woman and her dog?"

"Yes." At least he should be. This was a robber she was searching for, not a five-year-old girl. The man would be desperate and might be armed.

"She's sure a little thing," the officer said.

Jared agreed with a nod.

"Cute as all get out."

He agreed with that too.

With a squeal of tires, Jared pulled out of the lot and ignored the speed limit as he drove to the north side of town. He knew when he'd found the right place. In the gravel drive by the CIPs electrical power station was a dirty white Pontiac, with one fender crumpled and a front tire in shreds. Parked all around it were state police cars.

And uniformed officers.

As soon as Jared got out of his car, one stopped him. "You'll have to leave, sir," the man said.

"I'm with Laurie Crawford. The woman with the search dog." And there was no way he was leaving without her.

The officer gave him the same quizzical look the one at the bank had, and Jared realized a navy pin-striped suit, blue-and-white-striped shirt, and red-and-white tie did not look like a search-and-rescue uniform. "She left a message for me to meet her here," he added. "I didn't have time to change." He pulled her note from his pocket and waved it in front of the officer, then quickly stuffed it back in his pocket. He didn't want the man actually reading what Laurie had said.

He was getting pretty good at telling lies, he mused, *and it seemed to work*. The officer nodded toward a knot of people across the road and near the grandstand. "Talk to them."

Jared thanked the officer and hurried into the fairground area, toward the group of men and women standing by the grandstand. One was speaking into a two-way radio. As Jared neared the group, he could hear the transmission coming from the radio.

"I think we got him cornered," a man's voice said. "The dog keeps wanting to go over to some old bales of hay. The woman's holding him back, and—"

Jared heard a twang, both over the radio and in the distance, then the swearing. "Damn, the guy's shooting at us."

There was another sharp twang, like the crack of a whip. The voice coming through the radio turned panicky. "She's gone down."

That was all Jared needed to hear. Taking off at a dead run, he headed straight for the barn at the far end of the fairground. Voices yelling for him to stop didn't slow him. Only one thought drove him forward. Laurie had been shot. His Laurie. The woman he loved.

He easily shook off the first pair of hands that grabbed his arms. The second pair he jerked away from. It took a tackle to the knees to bring him down.

The ground was hard and gravelly, and it wasn't Officer Friendly on his back. "Hold it right where you are!" were the man's clipped orders.

It was difficult to do otherwise, his arm being jackknifed to his shoulder blade, a bony knee in his spine. Nevertheless Jared struggled to get up. "Laurie's been shot!" he exclaimed.

"And you're not moving until we know exactly what's going on."

Which took forever, as far as Jared was concerned. Uniformed men and women ran around back of the barn, guns drawn. Others yelled orders. And the three policemen holding him down kept asking the same questions. Who was he? Why was he running away from them? And what was he doing there?

"I've got to get to Laurie," he repeated, desperate to make them understand. "I work with her. She's my partner." And she could be dying.

Or dead.

With Joann he'd known she would die someday. They'd talked about it. Faced it. Cherished every day they had together. But Laurie . . .

She was young and vibrant. Healthy. The woman he loved. And he'd never told her that.

Then he saw her. She strode around the side of the barn grinning, patting her dog and digging her fingers into the Captain's thick ruff. Beside her was a young male police officer, who was looking at her as though she were made of pure gold. She laughed at something he said, then again patted her dog.

She was alive and happy, Jared thought, *and being hustled.* And he was livid. The moment the men holding him down released him, he stood and brushed off his trousers. Standing where he was, he waited, wondering if his eyes were actually flashing blue sparks.

"What the hell do you think you're doing?" he shouted before she was halfway to him.

She stopped, first recognition then surprise showing on her face. "Jared, what are you doing here?"

"Shouldn't that be my question? Aren't you supposed to be in Norton running a pet shop right now? Instead I find you playing cops and robbers. Getting yourself shot at."

She stiffened. "I was doing my job."

"You're qualified for search and rescue. Your job is to find lost people. Kids. Old people. Accident victims. It is not your job to go around risking your life."

"I don't limit the kind of calls I take. I go where I'm needed." She walked directly toward him, the Captain right by her side.

"Does that include going after . . . ? After—?" He waved his hand toward the scruffy, handcuffed punk the police were shoving into a patrol car. "After criminals?"

"If I want." There was a steely edge to her tone.

"Why? Do you like getting shot at? Is that it? Does it give you a thrill?" He simply couldn't understand her attitude. "Grow up, Laurie! People can get killed doing this."

She stopped directly in front of him, her body as tense as a coiled spring, her eyes a smoldering brown. He knew she was angry, yet he couldn't stop himself from going on. "Dammit, Laurie, I thought you'd been shot."

"I have been."

He quickly looked down her front. There were no signs of blood.

"Shot down by you," she added. Stepping away from him, she and her dog headed straight for the officer in charge.

Laurie didn't speak to him again the rest of the time they were in Harrisburg. The Captain was the hero of the day, Laurie the sweetheart. By the time she drove off, she and her dog had been photographed and interviewed by the *Daily Register*, filmed by both WSIL, Harrisburg, and KBSI, Carbondale, for the eleven-o'clock news, and hustled by several of the police officers. That she turned them all down didn't vanquish the jealousy twisting through Jared.

He followed her back to Norton. He knew she would have locked him out of her house if he hadn't had a key. She was certainly locking him out of her life with her stony glares and icy silence. Finally, before she escaped to her bedroom, he grabbed her arm.

The moment he touched her, the Captain

growled. It was a low, guttural sound that came from deep within the dog's throat. Under other circumstances Jared would have taken heed. Today he was too upset to tolerate it. "You stay out of this," he told the dog. "Go lie down."

To his surprise the Captain did.

"Oh, great," Laurie said. "Even my dog turns traitor." She tried to shake Jared's hand from her arm.

"I am not a traitor."

"No, you're worse." Her eyes narrowed. "How could you do that to me?"

He didn't ask what. He knew. He'd embarrassed her in front of the police and everyone around, and he was sorry, but it was too late to change things. "I didn't mean to. My God, Laurie, I thought you'd been shot. I thought I'd lost you."

"Well, you have."

She said it with such cold control, he was afraid he truly had. Releasing her, he let his arms fall to his sides. "I love you."

"Oh, sure. You know, someone else used to say that . . . always after he'd totally humiliated me."

"Let me guess. Greg."

"Right."

"He called today."

"So? He calls all the time."

Jared hadn't realized that. Greg had never called when he was around. "What do you two talk about?"

"We don't. I bought an answering machine so that I wouldn't have to talk to him. Greg usually just leaves messages. Now, get out of here. Out of my house and out of my life."

"I'm not going."

"It's over between us."

Her words devastated him, but the slight tremble of her lower lip gave him hope. "Laurie—"

"Laurie, nothing. I will not be treated like a

child. Never again." Tears were welling in her eyes, and her voice cracked.

"You've got to understand," he said. "Sometimes when people are scared, they say things they shouldn't. I was scared. Scared silly."

"So am I." She seemed to pull into herself, become even smaller and more vulnerable, and one tear did slip down her cheek. She wiped it away, took a deep breath, and the bold, undaunted Laurie Crawford resurfaced. "Maybe it's time I tell you about Greg."

"I wish you would."

"He used to treat me like a child, tell me what I could and could not do. It took me a long time to grow up enough to stand up to him. Too long. I don't want to go back to that kind of a relationship."

"I wouldn't want us to have that kind of a relationship. And I know you wouldn't let it happen. Maybe it took you a long time to grow up, but you did. You're too strong, too determined to ever let a man rule your life."

Only, that was what he'd tried to do, he realized. It bothered him to see the similarities between himself and Greg. Turning away, he walked into the living room. The newspapers on the couch had to be pushed aside, but he cleared a place and sat next to the Captain. He was determined to stay and talk this out with Laurie.

"Why did you even come to Harrisburg?" she asked, a longing to go back in time inherent in the question.

"Because the idea of you taking chances petrifies me, Laurie. I lost one woman I loved. I tried to keep her alive, watched over her as closely as I could, but still . . ."

"I don't have a weak heart."

"Maybe not, but you're not immortal." He reached down and scratched the Captain behind the ears. "I heard that shot and I thought I'd lost you."

Her gaze dropped to her dog. "I heard that shot and I thought I was going to lose him. I literally threw myself on him. Poor baby." For the first time since they'd entered the house, she grinned. "I think Cappie thought I'd gone crazy."

"We humans do crazy things when we're scared for someone we love. I'm sorry, Laurie. If I could redo today, I would."

"So would I." She walked toward him, slowly, hesitantly.

"Give me a second chance?"

"I gave Greg a second chance. Several second chances. I suppose I owe you at least one."

He made room for her on the sofa. "Tell me more about him."

She grimaced. "My relationship with Greg isn't something I like to talk about."

Jared knew that. In the weeks they'd known each other, she had been tight-lipped, almost secretive, about her ex-husband. Any attempt to bring up the man's name ended with her changing the subject. But today Jared was determined to learn everything. "You said you were married three years."

"Well, that's not exactly right. I think I said Greg and I lived together for three years."

Which probably meant she'd lived with him before they were married. Not that it mattered. He was no prude. "And you've been divorced . . . ?"

"Six years."

"So you were twenty when you started living with him?"

"No."

That stopped his hand on the dog's head. He'd thought he had it figured right.

"Greg and I were married two weeks after I turned sixteen."

"You were married at sixteen!" Surprise didn't begin to describe what he felt. "But that makes—"

"Makes me a fool." She sighed and explained. "I married Greg when I was sixteen. For two years he treated me like a child, which was exactly what I was. Every time we'd have an argument, I'd take off . . . go home to Mommy or to a friend's. Then after a while I'd go back to Greg and play the role he expected—the docile and obedient little girl. It took until after my eighteenth birthday before I really left.

"That time I went to California and lived with an aunt. I was ready to grow up. I went to night school and finished high school, worked and went to San Jose State. I didn't finish because I ran out of money, but while I was there, I took a psych class that convinced me I needed to face my past. So, at age twenty-two, I came back to Chicago. I was going to get a divorce and start my life over. But Greg asked—no, he begged—for another chance. So I gave him one. I thought I was all grown up and ready to handle an adult relationship. Next thing I knew, he was being his usual domineering, possessive self and I was acting like a little kid again."

"So you left him again."

"Yes. But I was through running away. Or so I thought. I filed for divorce, found a place of my own, and bought Cappie." The dog perked his ears at the sound of his name. "However, that didn't stop Greg from dropping by, 'just to see how I was doing.' And to make a few suggestions regarding the way I should live my life. I'd divorced him, but he felt he still had an obligation to run my life. So when Ruth started talking about moving back here, even though I'd sworn I wasn't going to take off again, I did. And that's my story."

"But he keeps calling."

"At least twice a month, sometimes more often."

"And you never talk to him?"

"Rarely. Oh, on his birthday. Christmas. Times like that I'll talk to him."

"He doesn't come see you?"

"No, Greg doesn't like to drive long distances. When he was younger, he was in a car accident. He had a bad case of whiplash, and even though he worked out and built up his neck and shoulder muscles, driving for any length of time still bothers him."

"What about your parents? Why did they ever let you get married at such a young age? Let you keep going back to him?"

"My father died when I was fourteen. That turned Mom's life upside down, and mine too. For a long time neither of us was functioning rationally. Plus, I loved Greg and would have lived with him, whether I was married to him or not. I think Mom just decided it was better to go along with the marriage idea than to fight it."

"Do you still love him?"

He expected her to say no, but her silence hurt. Glancing down at her dog, she pursed her lips the way she always did when thinking. Finally she answered. "I guess I'd have to say yes. Not the way I did when I was sixteen, or the way a woman should love a husband. But I do love Greg"—she looked at Jared—"maybe like a father."

"And will you go back to him again?" He had to know.

This time she didn't hesitate. "No, I'll never go back. It's where I'm headed that scares me."

It scared him too. He didn't want to lose her. The anger was behind them, but he knew he'd lost some of her trust. Reaching over, he took her hand. "I hope you're headed in the same direction I am."

Eleven

The direction they headed was her bedroom. Talk turned to kisses, and Jared became a firm believer in the saying that half the fun of fighting was the making up. They "made up" quite well.

The next morning he was aware of her before he even opened his eyes. Aware of the warmth of her leg between his, the womanly smell of her body, the tickle of her hair near his nose. She sighed and snuggled closer, still lost in the world of dreams. Small, slender fingers played across his chest, her touch going deep within him to stir an unquenchable need.

The soft haze of early morning greeted his blinking eyes. He focused on the photographs on the walls, on the snapshots of Laurie's mother with her father, her mother and her stepfather, her mother with her, and her father with her. There were none of Greg. Laurie had said she'd destroyed all of them, and Jared was glad. He was willing to share her with her family, but he wanted her to forget past mistakes. Their future depended on it.

She was beautiful in sleep, her mouth relaxed in

a half smile, long, dusky lashes resting lightly on unblemished cheeks. Sun-bleached streaks gilded her golden-brown hair, and its tousled disarray reminded him of their lovemaking the night before. She was probably getting tired of him dragging her into bed every time she looked at him with those big brown eyes of hers, but he couldn't get enough of her. He knew he never would.

Love, contentment, and protectiveness—they were all feelings she inspired in him. The love he gave freely, the contentment he enjoyed, but he was going to have to quell his desire to protect her. His protectiveness had almost ruined everything for them.

Her hand moved lower, her fingers splaying over his abdomen. He sucked in his stomach and tried to stop his rising need for her. His body didn't seem to understand good intentions, though. Fighting his desire for Laurie was a constant losing battle.

He couldn't stop a groan.

"You okay, Jared?"

He hadn't realized she was awake. She was looking up at him, concern marking her fine features. "I'm all right," he said. "Just having a hard time waking up."

Her hand dropped lower to surround his turgid length. "You are having a *hard* time, aren't you? Maybe I can make things a little less hard."

"Laurie?" He covered her hand with his. "You don't have to."

She let go, and he felt relieved and bereft. Telling her he could abstain was one thing; convincing his body was another. Especially with her so close.

Especially when she snuggled even closer, rubbing her hips against his, the soft, springy hairs between her legs caressing him. She arched her back, and her breasts teasingly touched his chest.

"Vixen," he growled.

"Something wrong?"

Wrong? Could one solitary man stop the world from spinning? His entire body vibrated with yearning. She needed protection, all right. Protection from him.

"Are you ready to get up?" The low pitch of her voice was seductive, and she made no move to rise. The only movement she made was her hands skimming over his back and down his sides, and her thigh rubbing along the insides of his.

"Laurie, if you really want to get up, I suggest you jump out of this bed and run like hell for your bathroom."

"Or? What will you do to me?"

"The same thing I did to you last night . . . and the night before, and the night before that. I was going to give you a break."

"Maybe I don't want a break. Ever think of that?" Her hand played between his legs. "I think I like getting you up in the morning."

She ran her fingertips around the most sensitive part of his body, and he sucked in a breath. "Well, you've certainly succeeded."

Almost hungrily she licked her lips. "Did I ever tell you, you have the most sexy blue eyes I've ever seen, Mr. North?"

"It's not my eyes that are sexy."

"Maybe it's your voice. I think I'm a sucker for a Southern drawl."

"I don't have a Southern drawl," he drawled.

She laughed—softly, lightly—then whispered in his ear, "Jared, make love to me."

That he could do. With his heart and soul, and in a hundred little ways. He made love to her with kisses feathered over her cheeks; by taking her mouth and parrying with her tongue. Everything he'd learned about her in the past few weeks he used to bring her pleasure. Their gentle touches and soft caresses fanned the fire between them, and sweat created a sheen on her skin and his, made their bodies silky smooth. Fingers communicated, boldly and intensely—holding, stroking, penetrating.

He kissed her breasts, delighting in the way they felt when he cupped them in his hands, the way a few licks with his tongue could change rosy nubs into rigid peaks. He knew her body well, yet it continued to be a mystery to him, so small and so resilient. So accommodating. So marvelous.

An arch of her hips, a slow rotation, and he was beyond reason. He took a moment for her protection, then they became one, in body and spirit, moving together, each the counterpart to the other. She was his and he was hers.

"Look at me," he commanded, and she opened her eyes.

"We belong together." He knew it as truly as night went with day. "Now, today, tomorrow, and forever."

"Together," she repeated in a hoarse whisper, entwining her legs with his.

"Forever."

The rhythmic, undulating motion of her hips carried him like a wave, rocking him from crest to crest. His tempo quickened as a liquid heat flowed through him. The only reality he knew were sensations, the only sounds the squeak of the bed and their ragged breathing.

"Oh, yes," she cried, her body tensing, shuddering.

He reared back, the moment right, and exploded into a pulsating release of pleasure. Morning had come. The sun had risen, and the world was in its proper orbit.

Ten minutes later Jared silently debated whether he should take a shower first or make coffee. As Laurie lay contentedly against his side, they both heard the Captain whine outside the closed bedroom door.

"He wants out," she said. "Guess it's really time to get up."

The bed felt empty the moment she left. Rolling to his side, Jared grinned as he watched her slip into the blue-and-white-striped dress shirt he'd worn the day before. The shoulders fell halfway down her arms, the cuffs dangled far below her fingertips, and the shirttail nearly reached her knees. Hastily she rolled the sleeves up to her elbows and buttoned two buttons, enough to give the illusion of propriety. Considering how much leg the cut of the shirt exposed, along with a most enticing cleavage, it was definitely an illusion.

"I'll let him out and put on the coffee," she said. "By the way, did I tell you Tina, my other part-time worker, called yesterday? An aunt or someone died, and she won't be coming in today."

Laurie dipped close to give him a quick kiss. He did like the view down the front of that shirt.

"Anyway, partner," she went on, "looks like either you or I are going to have to work today. Donna can't handle it all alone."

The Captain whined again, and she turned away, but Jared's fingers around her wrist stopped her from escaping. "We need to talk about the pet shop . . . and about us."

A flicker of concern shadowed her eyes, then she grinned. "Whatever you say, partner."

He could follow her progress through the house, starting right outside the bedroom with the hugs and words of affection she gave her dog, to the click of the back door as she let the Captain out, to the sound of running water in the kitchen. Stretching lazily, he wondered what more a man could ask for. He'd made love with the women he loved and would soon have a hot cup of coffee. Life was complete. He didn't even miss not having a cigarette.

During breakfast Jared broached the subject of the pet shop. He saw her tense as he asked, "When was the last time you had a Saturday you didn't have to work?"

"Eons ago. Jared, I know it seems like all I do is work at the shop or train Cappie, but what else can I do? It takes time and a lot of hard work for a new business to get started."

And most fail in the first five years, he thought. "Which do you prefer, running the pet shop or your search-and-rescue work?"

"My work with Cappie of course. But that costs money. At least with the pet shop, I have a chance of making some money."

He'd known which she would choose, had banked on it. "I remember you once said you'd like to train search-and-rescue teams."

"Sure, when I win the lottery. Even if people paid me for the training, I'd be in the poorhouse in a month. My two attempts to work with teams have failed miserably. Peter's wife is afraid to let him near me, and Diana has decided to live in Paris."

"What if you didn't have to worry about making money? What if you had enough to live on and could devote your time to training dogs and their handlers?"

"I'd be in heaven." She eyed him warily. "What are you getting at, Jared?"

He had to word this carefully. He was sure she loved him; her trust was the problem. "I think we should sell the pet shop and house, get your money and mine out of it. Then I think we should look at some property outside of town, somewhere where the zoning would allow you to run some obedience and training classes. And . . ."

Fear held back his words. Maybe it was better

simply to leave things as they were for a while, not chance a refusal.

Only Laurie wasn't content to let the matter hang. "And what? What's the catch to all this?"

He finished his proposal. "And marry me."

"And?" she prodded, motioning with her hand, as though expecting more.

It wasn't the reaction he'd expected. Where was the gasp of surprise? The squeal of delight? The hugs? The kisses? "Isn't marrying me enough?" he asked, more than a little affronted. And disappointed.

"Not when I know there's more." No emotions showing on her face, she started stacking their plates and clearing an area in front of her. "Why this sudden interest in helping me set up a training school, Jared? Why the offer to pay my bills? It wouldn't have anything to do with what happened yesterday, would it?"

"I love you. That's why I want to marry you."

"What if we do sell the pet shop, buy some land, and get married? What happens the next time I get a call to go after a bank robber? Do I have a husband telling me I can't go, that it's not safe? Is that the price I pay for getting to train tracking dogs?"

He didn't know how to answer her. No, he didn't want her doing any more felony searches. But to tell her that would spell certain death for their relationship.

The doorbell rang, and he thanked Providence for the reprieve. "I'll get it," he said, and pushed back his chair. "We can talk about this later."

The moment he opened the door, Jared decided it wasn't a reprieve Providence had sent. Dumbfounded, he stared at the man standing on the doorstep. His gaze went first to hair that would have once been blond and quite thick but was now nearly white and thinning in back, then to eyes as blue as cornflowers. The man wasn't very tall, probably five-eight or nine, and his waistline hung over his belt, but his shoulders were broad and the T-shirt he was wearing showed off arm muscles that were still quite firm.

Although it wasn't exactly like looking at a mirror image, there were enough similarities to send a chill down Jared's back. He knew without question that the man standing in front of him was Greg Crawford. He also knew Laurie hadn't told him everything about her ex-husband.

Greg Crawford was at least fifty years old.

"You the fiancé?" Greg asked, looking past Jared.

"You could say that," he said, though he knew Laurie wouldn't. He should have kept his mouth shut the day before.

From behind him came Laurie's soft voice. "Hello, Greg."

Stepping back, Jared let the man in. Jealousy and a cold dread gripped his insides as he watched Greg look Laurie over. During breakfast, having her dressed in his shirt had seemed sexy. Now he wished she were wearing a full-length, neck-high robe.

Greg grinned. "I see you still like to play dress-up."

Laurie wasn't smiling. "That's me, Greg, always the kid. But then that's the way you wanted it, wasn't it?"

"I've changed, honey. I won't treat you like a child anymore. Not if you don't want me to."

"I've changed, too, Greg." She backed up as he stepped toward her. "I'm not coming back to you. Not again. I told you that six years ago."

"You're still my little girl."

"Not anymore, Greg."

"Oh, God, Laurie. What am I going to do?"

Jared didn't know what to do himself when the

man started crying, but what bothered him most was that Laurie walked over to Greg and put her arms around him, patting him on the back and telling him it was all right. Jared was about to remind them both that he was still there, when she looked his way. "Could you get Greg some coffee, please? I think he needs it."

Reluctantly Jared did.

By the time he came back, she'd taken Greg into the living room, and they were seated on the couch. Greg was smoking a cigarette, and Laurie was holding his hand, talking to him softly, lovingly. She smiled when Jared held the mug out to her. "Good. Thanks. Greg, have some coffee while I get dressed. Then we'll talk."

The Captain sat directly in front of Greg, keeping a watchful eye on him, but Jared followed Laurie into the bedroom. She'd barely closed the door and shrugged out of his shirt when he exploded. "Why didn't you tell me he was old enough to be your father?"

"Because I thought you'd think I was stupid enough as it was, getting married at sixteen, leaving Greg, going back to him, leaving him and going back to him again."

"And what about us? That was quite a shock, standing there looking at a near twin. Do you have this thing for blonds with blue eyes and muscles?"

Laurie forgot the underwear she was pulling out of the drawer and spun around to face him. "You talk about shocks. I can't tell you what a shock it was when I first met you. Looking at you, it—it was like going back in time. You were even the same age Greg was when we got married."

"So is that it, I'm another father figure for you?"

She glared at him, then hastily pulled on her underpants.

"Why, Laurie? Why marry a man old enough to be your father?"

"Maybe because I needed a father. Maybe because I loved him." A pair of jeans went on, the zipper coming up with a decisive zip. "Maybe it wasn't logical, but at the time I was only sixteen. Any other questions?"

"Dozens."

"Do you think they could wait until after we get Greg out of here?" As she pulled a lightweight sweatshirt over her head, her words were muffled. Then she shook her hair loose and looked at him.

Jared shrugged and grabbed his shirt from where she'd tossed it on the bed. "I guess so."

They returned to the living room together, both properly dressed, his shirt now on his back and scented faintly with her aroma. Laurie sat on the end of the couch opposite Greg. The Captain moved to her side, laying his big head on her lap. She absently scratched the dog. Jared positioned himself in the chair directly across from Greg. If he looked proprietary, he didn't care.

"Did you drive?" she asked Greg.

"Yes. I left yesterday evening and drove to Mount Vernon, then it got dark and I stopped. Left early this morning and came straight here." He looked at Jared, and Jared knew it was their telephone conversation that had prompted Greg to take to the road. "I wanted to see how my little girl was doing."

Laurie stiffened perceptibly. "I'm doing fine. I don't need you checking up on me."

"Honey—" Again Greg looked at Jared, then back at Laurie. "Do we have to talk in front of him?"

The phone rang just then. Laurie glanced at Jared, silently asking him to get it, and grumbling, he rose from his chair.

He let the call go onto the answering machine. Those who knew Laurie expected it, and if it wasn't a call he wanted to take, he wasn't going to pick it up. He wanted to keep an eye on Laurie and Greg.

Greg had already tried to move closer to her, only the Captain's position between them kept him from getting too close. And the dog was watching the man, not in an aggressive or threatening way, but Jared had a feeling Greg understood that the dog was protecting her. Jared knew how long it had taken the Captain to accept him as a part of Laurie's life, and for once he was glad the shepherd was possessive of his mistress.

A man's voice came out of the answering machine. "Laurie, this is Undersheriff Garwood, from Chester. Saw you on television last night . . . how you helped the police over in Harrisburg. If you get this message in time, we sure could use you and your dog today."

Jared picked up the telephone. "Hold on. I'll get her for you."

He held the receiver out so that she could see it and called into the living room. "It's Undersheriff Garwood, from Chester. They need you and Cappie."

She left the couch immediately and took the call. Jared leaned against the doorjamb, where he could watch Greg and still listen to her conversation. Her side of it wasn't much. A yes, a no, and an "I understand." The rest of the time she listened or took notes.

Greg stood and paced restlessly, lighting another cigarette, then rubbing the back of his neck. He looked toward the kitchen often, always glaring when his gaze met Jared's. As Laurie hung up, Greg walked toward them.

"Two Honorees walked away last night," she said. "They were last seen going into a wooded area near the Mississippi River. The sheriff's department has two K-Nine teams on the scene this morning, but there's been a report of a sighting in another area, quite a ways south of there, and they'd like to use Cappie and me to check it out."

"Honorees?" Greg asked, giving her a questioning look. "What do you mean?"

"Prisoners. Men who are sometimes allowed beyond the confines of the prison."

"Criminals?" Greg shook his head. "Call him back and tell him you're not going."

Was that how he sounded? Jared wondered. Dictatorial. Unyielding. Like a father ordering his daughter not to do something.

She turned to him. "And what do you say, Jared?"

He wanted to put his arms around her, hold her close and safe, but he knew there were times when to hold something, you had to let it go. Now was one of those times. "It's your decision."

"Laurie, don't be foolish," Greg said in a chiding tone.

She ignored him, her gaze still on Jared's face. "Would you get my bag while I get ready?"

"May I go along?"

She didn't have a chance to answer. Greg moved closer, his voice rising. "You're not listening to me."

Turning to face him, she put a hand on his arm. "You're wrong, Greg. I have been listening to you. For the last six years I've been listening to you and telling you it's over between us. Now it's time you listen to me.

"You're a kind, wonderful man, Greg, but I don't want you making my decisions for me, or telling me what I can or cannot do. Not anymore. Do you understand?"

She started to walk away, but it was his turn to stop her. "You're not coming back this time, are you?"

Her hand covered his, and her words were gentle. "No, I'm not."

"I guess . . ." He looked at Jared. "I guess after I talked to him yesterday, I knew that. I just had to see you one more time, hear it from you."

"I told you I wasn't coming back six years ago."

"So you did." He sighed, then hugged her. "You'll always be my little girl, you know. Will you write? Let me know what you're doing? How you're doing?"

"I will."

Again he looked at Jared. There were tears in Greg's eyes. "Take good care of her."

She never did exactly say he could go with her. But then again she didn't say he couldn't. So when she was ready to leave the house, dressed in her usual uniform, Jared was also ready. He'd changed into a pair of jeans, a T-shirt, and the hiking boots he kept at her place. On the way to her car he grabbed a windbreaker from the trunk of his Cadillac, where it had been since late spring. In September one never knew what to expect of the weather. At the moment the sun had a warm glow and the wind was light, but the smell of fall was in the air, and there was no telling how long they might be out.

For a while they drove in silence. Jared wasn't sure what to say. He had more questions he wanted to ask about Greg, yet he was afraid of the answers he might hear. It was Laurie who finally brought up the subject.

"Daddy and Greg used to work together," she said without preamble. "I remember the first time Daddy brought him to the house. I had just turned thirteen and I thought he was the most perfect man alive. I spent days and nights dreaming that one day he'd look at me and realize I wasn't really a shy, awkward little girl but the woman he loved."

Jared could understand her feelings. "When

Becky was that age, she was always fawning all
over the salesmen and clients Dad would bring to
the house. She'd never say a word, but she'd follow
them around and gaze at them, all moon-eyed.
Dad wanted me to talk to her, but I told him just to
ignore it and she'd outgrow it. She did."

Laurie nodded. "If my father hadn't died right
after my fourteenth birthday, I probably would
have outgrown my fantasy too. But Daddy did die,
and Greg started coming over, spending more and
more time with me. He was worried about the way
Mom was staying out so late at night. He'd hold me
close and let me cry and would tell me everything
was going to be all right."

"Did Greg ever . . ." Jared wasn't sure how to
phrase it. "Ever do anything to you?"

"You mean, did he sexually molest me?" She
glanced his way and laughed lightly. "No, just the
opposite. Other than hugs and kisses, he never
touched me until after we were married. In fact I
don't think, at first, that Greg ever meant our
relationship to be anything more than father-
daughter. He'd been married before, and he and
his wife had tried for years to have children. When
his wife finally did get pregnant, something went
wrong during the delivery. I'm not exactly sure
what, he never wanted to talk about it, but his wife
died, along with their baby daughter."

"So he became your father, and you were his
little girl."

"That was about it."

"What about after you two were married? You
didn't have any children. Did you . . . ?"

"Have sex?" she finished for him. "Yes. But not
very often." Her sidelong glance was warm. "In bed,
there's absolutely no similarities between you two,
except that he was always as careful as you are
that I wouldn't get pregnant.

"Still, the problem in our marriage was never sex, or the lack of it. It was his attitude. His need to tell me what I could and could not do. His need to protect me. It's the same problem I see with us, and it's the reason I can't marry you."

Twelve

"You can't marry me?" An icy chill ran down Jared's spine.

She nodded. "This morning you wanted to say exactly the same thing Greg said. I could see it on your face, the way you stiffened the moment I mentioned prisoners."

"Is it wrong to be concerned about your safety? I love you, Laurie. How would you feel if I were the one who was in danger?"

"But I won't be in any danger. It's not like these men are armed. They're Honorees. Trustees."

"And they've escaped." Either she didn't see the potential danger or she was ignoring it.

"The sheriff isn't going to put me in a dangerous position. They just want to use Cappie to check out this other sighting. If it is the men, the K-Nine Corps will take over."

Jared wasn't convinced, but the firm thrust of her jaw told him it was no use arguing. Pigheadedness and determination obviously weren't determined by size. It was either join her or lose her. "Think they'll let me help?"

• • •

No one objected, and Jared was teamed up with Laurie, the Captain, and Sheriff's Deputy Roy Whitman. After a briefing they were given direction to the area where a fisherman had described two men who fit the escapees' descriptions. Although it was doubtful the prisoners had gotten that far south of Chester, the possibility had to be checked out.

Laurie and the Captain got into the back of the patrol car while Jared grabbed his jacket and Deputy Whitman received last-minute instructions. Ten minutes later they were at the site where the fisherman had reported the sighting. The prison had provided a piece of clothing that belonged to one of the escapees. Laurie let the Captain get a good scent off it, then gave him the command to track.

Following the shepherd, they spread out to cover the greatest amount of territory. There were no opportunities for long conversations, but Jared could tell that Deputy Whitman considered the assignment a waste of time. "He's not finding anything, is he?" the younger man yelled to Laurie.

The Captain was trotting ahead of her, windscenting. "He hasn't shown any signs that he's picked up on anything."

"I told the sheriff he wouldn't. There's no way those two could have gotten down here. Not unless they're half fish. Betcha our dogs make a find within the hour."

It would be good news to Jared if they did. Laurie and he needed to talk, privately and without the distraction and tension a search. Since her proclamation that she couldn't marry him, a knot grew ever tighter in his stomach. She was afraid of repeating past mistakes. He had to convince her he was different from Greg. Only, could he?

Laurie strode purposefully across the field. She still reminded him of a hummingbird—constantly in motion, small and colorful, her orange pack and vest easy to follow. She took two steps to his one, yet he knew she could go for hours without tiring.

She was well trained, capable, and gutsy. How could he convince her that he respected her as a mature, competent woman, yet worried about her safety? Maybe he was a little overprotective of the women in his life, but he was trying to do better. Even Becky had commented recently that he was talking to her more like a friend than a big brother, and she liked it.

A future without Laurie was impossible for him even to consider.

Jared knew the moment the Captain picked up a scent. Hours of working with Laurie as she exercised, played with, and trained her dog had taught him a lot about how tracking dogs worked. When the Captain lost the scent and quartered back, Jared also understood what was happening. The escapees wouldn't have come out into the open, not unless they absolutely had to, so the scents the Captain was picking up were being carried by air currents from somewhere else. Considering the wind direction and terrain, it was logical for Laurie to order her dog into the woods.

Deputy Whitman called in their location. The other teams were also hot on a scent. With the sites so far apart, it seemed impossible the dogs were following the same men, yet Jared shared Laurie's trust in her dog's abilities. "If he says they're in there, they are," he told Whitman.

In the woods it was harder to walk. Branches and brush snagged at clothing, and Jared slipped on his jacket, more to protect his arms than for warmth. To his surprise there was a pack of cigarettes in one pocket, but he wasn't even tempted to grab a smoke. That was one habit he'd truly kicked.

He tried to keep an eye on Laurie, but it wasn't easy. The underbrush and growth were dense, and only occasionally did he glimpse the orange of her vest. Cigarettes were easy to give up compared with stifling the habit of worrying about someone he loved. He wasn't sure it could be done.

"He's definitely on a track," she called to Whitman.

"Has he ever had any felony-search training?" the deputy asked from his position between them.

"No. I told the sheriff that."

"Then be ready to call him off and let me go ahead. If this really is them, we want to get the other—"

Jared heard a dull thud, like the thunk of a dropped melon, and a grunt. From the deputy's direction branches snapped, and every muscle in Jared's body tensed. Sounds, shadows, the slightest movement grabbed his attention. "Whitman!" he yelled.

"Cappie!" Laurie called.

"Watch yourself," Jared warned her.

"No, you watch yourself," threatened a low, guttural voice from behind him.

Jared spun around to face a thin man, not more than five feet six inches in height, holding a shotgun. Like a cornered wild animal, the escapee was ready to fight for his freedom, and the look in his eyes said he'd use the gun if that was what it took. Jared stood perfectly still. "I'm watching."

A startled cry from Laurie's direction tore at his insides. There had been two escapees. He now knew where the other one was. "Laurie!" he screamed.

It was a man's voice that responded. "Got her."

The one with the gun nodded in the direction of Laurie's cry. "Start walking that way."

Jared would have run if the dense underbrush and fallen trees hadn't held him back. "If you've done anything to hurt her, so help me—"

"Just keep walking," the man behind him ordered.

The man holding Laurie captive was big and muscular, and any resistance on her part would have been as effective as a gnat battling a bull. She was standing tall, her chin raised, but Jared could read the fear in her eyes. On the ground lay Deputy Whitman, his eyes closed, blood running from a cut on the side of his head.

The Captain sat in front of Laurie, a low growl emanating from his throat, his eyes fixed on the massive hand gripping Laurie's small arm. The man's other arm was raised, a gnarled stick in his hand. He was poised and ready to hit the dog; nevertheless Jared had no doubt the shepherd would have attacked if not for Laurie's terse commands. "No. Sit, boy. Good boy."

Her gaze darted to the gun pointed at Jared, and her face paled. She looked small and helpless and terrified. "That's right, girl," the man behind Jared said. "You keep that old dog of yours nice and friendly. Otherwise I might just have to use this gun on your friend, here. You understand?"

Laurie nodded, her momentary glance at Jared telling him more than words ever could. She was as frightened for him as he was for her.

"Looks like maybe we found us a car and a couple of hostages," the one with the gun said.

"I wouldn't recommend that." Jared hoped he sounded more confident than he felt. "You're just going to make things worse for yourselves."

The big man holding Laurie laughed gruffly. "Hell, things can't get much worse. All we was gonna do was have ourselves a little night on the town, and that woman goes and tells on us. I ain't goin' back to the lockup."

"Is he dead?" The smaller man nudged the prone deputy with his foot.

"No, but I hit him pretty good. I don't think he's gonna be waking up for a while. I was gonna get his gun when she came runnin' up on me, then the dog."

The man let go of Laurie's arm and moved toward the deputy. His partner stopped him. "You can get his gun after you frisk this one."

They could do whatever they wanted to him, Jared thought. It was Laurie he was worried about. She continued talking to the Captain in low, soothing tones, telling him to stay. The dog listened to her, totally obedient. As the bigger man ran his hands over Jared's jacket and jeans, Jared tried to be equally successful in communicating with Laurie. He wanted her to run if she had a chance. Save herself. A slight shake of her head, barely discernible, gave him his answer. She was being stubborn, as usual.

And how he loved her.

"Hey, look what I found." The man pulled the pack of cigarettes from Jared's jacket pocket. "Just what you was saying you wished you had."

"Throw them here," the other man ordered.

"You got any matches?" his searcher asked Jared, patting his pockets.

"No, I quit last June. Those are old."

It didn't seem to bother the man with the gun. He tapped out a cigarette. "You got some matches, girly?"

Jared gave a small nod to her, looked down at the Captain, then back at her. He wasn't sure she caught his message. It was the gun that held her attention.

"Well, do ya?" the man repeated.

"Yes." The word was a sibilant rasp. Laurie didn't move. "They're in my gear bag."

"Well, get them." The gunman stuck the cigarette in his mouth and waited.

Slowly she dropped the pack from her shoulders and kneeled to open it, but her gaze stayed on Jared. The man beside him straightened, the results of his search producing one pocket knife, a wallet, and a set of car keys. Immediately he began going through the wallet. "We got us a Mister Jared Thacker North here." He hummed with satisfaction when he checked out the money and the credit cards. "Those kids may have supplied us with a gun and food, but this guy is gonna make life a little easier for a while."

Jared didn't pay attention to the money the man was taking from his wallet. He was more interested in the odds, and when only one of the two men was armed, the odds were better. "You know, smoking's a nasty habit," he said loudly.

Laurie froze. Her gaze darted from her dog, to the gun, then back to Jared. The Captain's ears perked forward, but he didn't move.

Give the command, Jared silently willed her, his gaze locked on her face. *Give it now, while this guy is busy going through my wallet.*

He could see her reluctance in her eyes, the internal war she was waging with her fear. He'd almost given up hope, when the man with the gun grew impatient. "Lady, are you gonna get those matches, or do I have to do it myself?"

He turned away from Jared, the gun no longer facing any of them, and Laurie spoke. "You know, smoking is a nasty habit."

Immediately the Captain and Jared went into action.

The dog flew through the air like a missile from a Deadeye slingshot, and Jared came around with a right upper cut that would have made Muhammad Ali envious. He felt the impact of his knuckles hitting the escapee's jawbone all the way up to his shoulder blade, and behind him he heard the hiss of air leaving the other man's lungs as the Captain's front paws and one hundred pounds of weight hit his chest. Laurie was also on the move, not running away to safety, but directly into the fracas.

"Get out of here!" Jared yelled, and ducked a wild swing.

Although muscle for muscle he and the bigger man looked to be fairly equally matched, Jared had no desire to test his fighting skills any further than he had. Literally using his head, he drove his forehead into the other man's solar plexus. The wind taken out of him, the escapee went down on his knees. It was then that Laurie took over.

"Stop!" she yelled, the finality of that one word emphasized by a blast from the shotgun.

She toppled down onto her back, her feet fanning the air, while the man Jared had hit coughed and wheezed and swore, and the other man continued gasping for air, the Captain standing square on his chest.

Help didn't take long in coming, and the sheriff willingly filled in some details. "We'd just come across two teenagers when we got your call. The boys were camping out, and I have a feeling they'd been doing or were planning on doing a little illegal squirrel hunting. These two jumped them just before dawn, tied them up, ate their food, and took their shotgun and boat."

"Only, from what the boys said," a handler from one of the other dog teams continued, "the boat wasn't the greatest. These guys probably got this far and decided they'd be better off on land."

"They must have thought they'd shaken anyone

trailing them," the other handler added. "And they would have, if that fisherman hadn't seen them."

"And Cappie hadn't picked up their scent." Laurie hugged her dog, burying her face in his thick black ruff. Jared had done the same thing, once the sheriff and his deputies arrived on the scene. And as soon as they got home, he was buying the dog the thickest steak in town.

"I didn't realize you were training him for felony search work," the first handler said. He was petting his own dog, but his gaze was on Laurie. "Aren't you too small for that?"

Jared didn't care how many men looked at her, as long as her eyes were on him. And they were. Grinning, she answered the tracker. "I'm both too small and not interested. Maybe it doesn't bother you guys to be shot at or to have a gun waved in your face, but I think I aged ten years in the last two days."

Jared would give himself at least that many years, too, and he wouldn't be surprised if his hair was now pure white. Laurie's decision pleased him, but he stood back, saying nothing. She had to know he wouldn't interfere again.

He really wasn't sure what her mood was, though. Talking to the sheriff, giving him the detailed report on the search, she was bubbly and animated, obviously proud of her dog and pumped with adrenaline. But whenever Jared caught her looking at him, he saw concern and apprehension. Their personal problems had not been resolved.

He offered to do the driving back to Norton, and she surprised him by agreeing. For the first ten miles she chattered on, bouncing between praising her dog to berating the prison system for being so trusting and parents for letting teenage boys take shotguns on camping trips. Jared didn't care what she talked about. He knew she was avoiding the one topic they needed to discuss—them.

When she at last fell silent, he tensed. Having a gun pointed at his back had been less frightening than what he knew was about to come. He hung on to the steering wheel with a death grip that turned his knuckles white and stared straight ahead, unwilling to initiate the conversation.

It was Laurie who did.

"You know, any time I go out with Cappie, even if it's just searching for a missing person, there's always an element of danger. The weather can be as great a foe as any man."

"I know." And he would be afraid for her every time she went out.

"And you can't always go with me."

"I know."

She sighed and leaned back against the seat, no longer looking at him. Her voice was softer, and her words came slower. "When I saw that gun pointed at you, I was scared."

"I—"

"Know," she finished with him, and laughed, reaching over to touch his arm. "Oh, Jared, what are we going to do?"

"Get married, have kids, and live happily ever after." He said it casually, but there was nothing casual about the way he felt.

"You're going to try to boss me around and shelter me, and it's going to make me madder than hell, and I'm not going to let you."

"Just don't run away."

"I won't. One thing I discovered was running doesn't get you anywhere. Shoot, even coming down here, what did I run into but a man who looked and acted enough like Greg to be his brother?"

He glanced at her. "I definitely don't see you as a daughter."

"And I don't see you as a father figure."

"You're sure?" He didn't want a child, he wanted a wife . . . a partner in life.

"I'm sure." Her fingers squeezed his arm. "Would you really foot the bills for a place to train search-and-rescue teams?"

"There's a farm not too far from Becky and Tom's place. The house will have to be remodeled, and I'll want a pool, but I think we could get a zoning variance so that you could give obedience classes and work with handlers and dogs. And once we're married, we can invite the guy with the Lab and his wife over. I'm sure I can convince her she has nothing to be jealous about. After that, who knows how many others will come to you for training. You said yourself there aren't that many search-and-rescue teams in this area."

"What about your beautiful home? And your father's advice about not investing in anything that—" She grinned. "Anything that made excreta."

"That house was right for my life with Joann. You and I need more space." He nodded toward the dog stretched out on the backseat. "Plus, he's almost six. You said yourself that a search-and-rescue dog's working years are limited. Which means you're going to need to get a puppy soon and start with its training. I really don't think puppies go well with white wool carpeting, velvet upholstery, and hardwood floors."

"You'd do that for me?" She stared at him with wonder in her eyes. And love. Momentarily easing his foot off the gas pedal, he leaned over and kissed her cheek. "Maybe we'll get two puppies. I kinda of like all this dog-training stuff, and North Machinery could probably keep running while its president was off on a search."

"Jared." She said his name with a throaty tremor, then her fingers slid down his arm to his hand. His knuckles were already puffy and turning purple. "My knight in shining armor. We're going to be a sorry couple tomorrow, you with your bruised hand—"

"And shoulder," he added. Those muscles were already stiffening up.

"Your bruised hand and shoulder and my bruised derriere. I never expected that gun to have the kick of a mule. I'll be lucky to get out of bed in the morning."

"Getting into bed sounds good to me."

"Jared . . ." This time when she said his name, his eyes widened. Her hand had left his to slip between his legs. "Let's send Donna home and close the pet shop today. Let's go to bed while we can still move."

In his youthful fantasies he'd once imagined picking up a hitchhiker and having her turn into a sex goddess who pleasured him as he drove. Laurie was no stranger he'd picked up, but she was definitely a sex goddess. He made it to her house in record time and was glad he wasn't pulled over for breaking the speed limit. It would have been hard to explain what the rush was. Then again, *hard* was the key word, and one look at the bulge behind his fly and any officer would have known where he was headed in such a hurry.

It seemed a lifetime since they'd woken in her bed to make love and greet the sunrise. The sheets were still rumpled and pulled back, and the scent of their lovemaking lingered in the room. Their clothing came off in seconds, then as he slid the scarf from her hair, freeing it, she wrapped her arms around his neck, pulling herself up on her toes and rubbing her body against his.

He loved it. Loved her.

"Ask me again," she begged.

"Ask you what?" He groaned as she dropped one hand down and skimmed her fingernails over his rigid manhood.

"To marry you."

"Do you want me to propose on bended knee?" He would, though he hated to move with her bare breasts teasing his chest and the curly brown hairs between her thighs tickling every ultrasensitive inch of him.

"No, you don't have to propose on bended knee. With us I want life to be one surprise after another."

And she did surprise him. Dropping to her own knees, she kissed him, and his hormones exploded as the fire of need flowed through his arteries. Threading his fingers into her hair, his head thrown back, he gasped the only sensible thought he could manage. "Oh, Laurie, please marry me."

The sun was setting when Jared realized she'd never answered his question. Rolling over and bracing himself on one arm, he picked up a lock of her hair and lazily trailed it over her cheek. Lashes that rested on cheeks still flushed with sexual delight fluttered, then rose. He could see himself in her eyes. Her smile came quickly and lovingly, and she reached up and touched her fingertips to his jaw.

"Will you marry me?" he asked one more time.

"Yes."

Outside the bedroom door the Captain barked, and Jared chuckled. "I think he just said, 'Finally.'"

THE EDITOR'S CORNER

What an irresistible line-up of romance reading you have coming your way next month. Truly, you're going to be **LOVESWEPT** by these stories that are guaranteed to heat your blood and keep you warm throughout the cold, winter days ahead.

First on the list is **WINTER BRIDE**, LOVESWEPT #522, by the ever-popular Iris Johansen. Ysabel Belfort would trade Jed Corbin anything for his help on a perilous mission—her return to her South American island home, to recover what she'd been forced to leave behind. But he demands her sensual surrender, arousing her with a fierce pleasure, until they're engulfed in a whirwind of danger and desire. . . . A gripping and passionate love story, from one of the genre's premier authors.

You'll be **BEWITCHED** by Victoria Leigh's newest LOVESWEPT, #523, as Hank Alton is when he meets Sally. According to his son, who tried to steal her apples, she's a horribly ugly witch, but instead Hank discovers a reclusive enchantress whose eyes shimmer with warmth and mystery. A tragedy had sent Sally Michaels in search of privacy, but Hank shatters her loneliness with tender caresses and burning kisses. Victoria gives us a shining example of the power of love in this touching romance guaranteed to bring a smile to your face and tears to your eyes.

Judy Gill creates a **GOLDEN WARRIOR**, LOVESWEPT #524, in Eric Lind, for he's utterly masculine, outrageously sexy, and has a rake's reputation to match! But Sylvia Mathieson knows better than to get lost in his bluer-than-blue eyes. He claims to need the soothing fire of her love, and she aches to feel the heat of his body against hers, but could a pilot who roams the skies ever choose to make his home in her arms? The sensual battles these two engage in will keep you turning the pages of this fabulous story from Judy.

Please give a big welcome to brand-new author Diane Pershing and her first book, **SULTRY WHISPERS**, LOVESWEPT #525. Lucas Barabee makes Hannah Green melt as he woos her with hot lips and steamy embraces. But although she wants the job he offered, she knows only too well the danger of mixing business with pleasure. You'll delight in the sweet talk and irresistible moves Lucas must use to convince Hannah she can trust him with her heart. A wonderful romance by one of our New Faces of '92!

In **ISLAND LOVER**, LOVESWEPT #526, Patt Bucheister sweeps you away to romantic Hawaii, where hard-driving executive Judd Stafford has been forced to take a vacation. Still, nothing can distract him . . . until he meets Erin Callahan. Holding her is like riding a roller coaster of emotions—all ups and downs and stomach-twisting joy. But Erin has fought hard for her independence, and she isn't about to make it easy for Judd to win her over. This love story is a treat, from beginning to end!

Laura Taylor has given her hero quite a dilemma in **PROMISES**, LOVESWEPT #527. Josh Wyatt has traveled to the home he's never known, intending to refuse the inheritance his late grandfather has left him, but executor Megan Montgomery is determined to change his mind. A survivor and a loner all his life, Josh resists her efforts, but he can't ignore the inferno of need she arouses in him, the yearning to experience how it feels to be loved at last. Laura has outdone herself in crafting a story of immense emotional impact.

Look for four spectacular books this month from FAN-FARE. Bestselling author Nora Roberts will once again win your praise with **CARNAL INNOCENCE**, a riveting contemporary novel where Caroline Waverly learns that even in a sleepy town called Innocence, secrets have no place to hide, and in the heat of steamy summer night it takes only a single spark to ignite a deadly crime of passion. Lucy Kidd delivers **A ROSE WITHOUT THORNS**, a compelling historical romance set in eighteenth-century England. Susannah Bry's world is turned upside-down when her father sends her to England to live with wealthy relatives, and she meets the bold and dashing actor Nicholas Carrick. New author Alexandra Thorne will dazzle you with the contemporary novel **DESERT HEAT**. In a world of fiery beauty, lit by a scorching desert sun, three very different women will dare to seize their dreams of glory . . . and irresistible love. And, Suzanne Robinson will captivate you with **LADY GALLANT**, a thrilling historical romance in the bestselling tradition of Amanda Quick and Iris Johansen. A daring spy in Queen Mary's court, Eleanora Becket meets her match in Christian de Rivers, a lusty, sword-wielding rogue, who has his own secrets to keep, his own enemies to rout—and his own brand of vengeance for the wide-eyed beauty whom he loved too well. Four terrific books from FANFARE, where you'll find only the best in women's fiction.

Happy Reading!

With warmest wishes for a new year filled with the best things in life,

Nita Taublib

Nita Taublib
Associate Publisher / LOVESWEPT
Publishing Associate / FANFARE

Enter Loveswept's Wedding Contest

AH! WEDDINGS! The joyous ritual we cherish in our hearts—the perfect ending to courtship. Brides in exquisite white gowns, flowers cascading from glorious bouquets, handsome men in finely tailored tuxedos, butterflies in stomachs, nervous laughter, music, tears, and smiles. . . . AH! WEDDINGS!! But not all weddings have a predictable storybook ending; sometimes they are much, much more— grooms who faint at the altar, the cherubic ring bearer who drops the band of gold in the lake to see if it will float, traffic jams that strand the bride miles from the church, or the gorgeous hunk of a best man who tempts the bride almost too far. . . . AGHH!! WEDDINGS!!!

LOVESWEPT is celebrating the joy of weddings with a contest for YOU. And true to LOVESWEPT's reputation for innovation, this contest will have THREE WINNERS. Each winner will receive a year of free LOVESWEPTs and the opportunity to discuss the winning story with a LOVESWEPT editor.

Here's the way it goes. We're looking for short wedding stories, real or from your creative imagination, that will fit in one of three categories:

1) THE MOST ROMANTIC WEDDING
2) THE FUNNIEST THING THAT EVER HAPPENED AT A WEDDING
3) THE WEDDING THAT ALMOST WASN'T

This will be LOVESWEPT's first contest in some time for writers and aspiring writers, and we are eagerly anticipating the discovery of some terrific stories. So start thinking about your favorite real-life wedding experiences—or the ones you always wished (or feared?) would happen. Put pen to paper or fingers to keyboard and tell us about those WEDDINGS (AH)!!

For prizes and rules, please see rules, which follow.

BANTAM LOVESWEPT WEDDING CONTEST
OFFICIAL RULES

1. *No purchase necessary.* Enter Bantam's LOVESWEPT WEDDING CONTEST by completing the Official Entry Form below (or handprinting the required information on a plain 3" x 5" card) and writing an original story (5–10 pages in length) about one of the following three subjects: (1) The Most Romantic Wedding, (2) The Funniest Thing That Ever Happened at a Wedding, or (3) The Wedding That Almost Wasn't. Each story must be typed, double spaced, on plain 8 1/2" x 11" paper, and must be headed on the top of the first page with your name, full address, home telephone number, date of birth, and, below that information, the title of the contest subject you selected when you wrote your story. You may enter a story in one, two, or all three contest categories, but a separate Entry Form or Card must accompany each entry, and each entry must be mailed to Bantam in a separate envelope bearing sufficient postage. Completed Entry Forms or Cards, along with your typed story, should be sent to:

   BANTAM BOOKS
   LOVESWEPT WEDDING CONTEST
   Department NT
   666 Fifth Avenue
   New York, New York 10103

   All stories become the property of Bantam Books upon entry, and none will be returned. All stories entered must be original stories that are the sole and exclusive property of the entrant.

2. *First Prizes (3).* Three stories will be selected by the LOVESWEPT editors as winners in the LOVESWEPT WEDDING CONTEST, one story on each subject. The prize to be awarded to the author of the story selected as the First Prize winner of each subject-matter category will be the opportunity to meet with a LOVESWEPT editor to discuss the story idea of the winning entry, as well as publishing opportunities with LOVESWEPT. This meeting will occur at either the Romance Writers of America convention to be held in Chicago in July 1992 or at Bantam's offices in New York City. Any travel and accommodations necessary for the meeting are the responsibility of the contest winners and will not be provided by Bantam, but the winners will be able to select whether they would rather meet in Chicago or New York. If any First Prize winner is unable to travel in order to meet with the editor, that winner will have an opportunity to have the First Prize discussion via an extended telephone conversation with a LOVESWEPT editor. The First Prize winners will also be sent all six LOVESWEPT titles every month for a year (approximate retail value: $200.00).

   Second Prizes (3). One runner-up in each subject-matter category will be sent all six LOVESWEPT titles every month for six months (approximate retail value: $100.00).

3. All completed entries must be postmarked and received by Bantam no later than January 15, 1992. Entrants must be over the age of 21 on the date of entry. Bantam is not responsible for lost or misdirected or incomplete entries. The stories entered in the contest will be judged by Bantam's LOVESWEPT editors, and the winners will be selected on the basis of the originality, creativity, and

writing ability shown in the stories. All of Bantam's decisions are final and binding. Winners will be notified on or about May 1, 1992. Winners have 30 days from date of notice in which to accept their prize award, or an alternative winner will be chosen. If there are insufficient entries or if, in the judges' sole opinion, no entry is suitable or adequately meets any given subject as described above, Bantam reserves the right not to declare a winner for either or both of the prizes in any particular subject-matter category. There will be no prize substitutions allowed and no promise of publication is implied by winning the contest.

4. Each winner will be required to sign an Affidavit of Eligibility and Promotional Release supplied by Bantam. Entering the contest constitutes permission for use of the winner's name, address, biographical data, likeness, and contest story for publicity and promotional purposes, with no additional compensation.

5. The contest is open to residents in the U.S. and Canada, excluding the Province of Quebec, and is void where prohibited by law. All federal and local regulations apply. Employees of Bantam Books, Bantam Doubleday Dell Publishing Group, Inc., their subsidiaries and affiliates, and their immediate family members are ineligible to enter. Taxes, if any, are the responsibility of the winners.

6. For a list of winners, available after June 15, 1992, send a self-addressed stamped envelope to WINNERS LIST, LOVESWEPT WEDDING CONTEST, Department NT, 666 Fifth Avenue, New York, New York 10103.

OFFICIAL ENTRY FORM

BANTAM BOOKS
LOVESWEPT WEDDING CONTEST
Department NT
666 Fifth Avenue
New York, New York 10103

NAME _____

ADDRESS _____

CITY _____ STATE _____ ZIP _____

HOME TELEPHONE NUMBER _____

DATE OF BIRTH _____

CONTEST SUBJECT FOR THIS STORY IS: _____

_____

SIGNATURE CONSENTING TO ENTRY _____

_____

FANFARE

On Sale in January

LIGHTS ALONG THE SHORE

☐ (29331-1) $5.99/6.99 in Canada
by Diane Austell

Marin Gentry would become a woman to be reckoned with -- but a woman who must finally admit how she longs to be loved. A completely involving and satisfying novel, and the debut of a major storyteller.

LAWLESS

☐ (29071-1) $4.99/5.99 in Canada
by Patricia Potter
author of RAINBOW

Willow Taylor held within her heart a love of the open frontier -- and a passion for a renegade gunman they called Lobo -- the lone wolf. Their hearts ran free in a land that was LAWLESS . . .

HIGHLAND REBEL

☐ (29836-5) $4.99/5.99 in Canada
by Stephanie Bartlett
author of HIGHLAND JADE

Catriona Galbraith was a proud Highland beauty consumed with the fight to save the lush rolling hills of her beloved home, the Isle of Skye. Ian MacLeod was the bold American sworn to win her love.

☐ Please send me the books I have checked above. I am enclosing $ _____ (please add $2.50 to cover postage and handling). Send check or money order, no cash or C. O. D.'s please.

Mr./ Ms. _____

Address _____

City/ State/ Zip _____

Send order to: Bantam Books, Dept. FN, 414 East Golf Road, Des Plaines, IL 60016

Please allow four to six weeks for delivery.

Prices and availablity subject to change without notice.

THE SYMBOL OF GREAT WOMEN'S FICTION FROM BANTAM

Ask for these books at your local bookstore or use this page to order.

FN 20 - 1/92